Wednesday Mourning

Mary Verwys

Wednesday Mourning

Mary Verwys

Second Printing 2004
Third Printing 2009
Fourth Printing 2018
Cover produced by Holland Litho Printing

LIBRARY OF CONGRESS CATALOGING-IN-PUBLICATION DATA

Verwys, Mary Waalkes

Wednesday Mourning/Mary Waalkes Verwys
p. cm.

ISBN 0-9317641-6-5

Abortion — Nonfiction. 2. Counseling — nonfiction. I. Title.

TX5.945.703 2003

Connect with the Garden of Hope Ministry

garden of hope — where mercy meets hope

Website: gardenofhope.com
Email: thegardenofhope@gmail.com
Denise: Post-Abortive Facilitator
616.724.0649 (call or text)

General Ministry Phone: 616.307.6646
Ministry Contact Address:
PO Box 888434
Grand Rapids, MI 49588

Dedication

This book is dedicated to

The God Of All HOPE

and

The dear sidewalk counselors of Grand Rapids, that faithfully display the mercy and compassion of God, to a hurting and desperate world.

The selection of the cover photo

The cover photo reminded me so much of the women we see each week, as we stand at the ready to help. Battling alone in those final steps as they approach the clinic doors. So unsettled with their set of circumstances. Overwhelmed with life. In heart-wrenching despair.

But it is us, too. The helpers. The burden-carriers. The mercy-givers. The grace-extenders. Head in hands, we beg The Father for intervention and rescue! We would do anything… ANYTHING…to lessen their load.

I've seen it a thousand times…women coming to the abortion clinic, still unsettled in their decision.

Despair. Shock. Grief.

"Where do I go from here? Where do I turn for help?
What will my life be like now? Will I ever be the same?"

I've heard it a thousand times…women coming to the abortion clinic, spewing out excuses for their decision.

Anger. Frustration. Hopelessness.

"But you don't understand! There is nothing else I can do!
I am all alone. It will be best for everyone."

I've felt it a thousand times...deep anguish as I watch a parade of unsuspecting women yield to the nightmare of their decision.

Sorrow. Horror. Mourning.

"Please don't! We will walk this journey with you!
There is so much help available! There is HOPE!"

God Have Mercy

Contents

Contents (continued)

Face To Face

Conversations On The Sidewalk

Introduction

For over thirty years I have counseled on the sidewalks in front of abortion clinics. As an eyewitness, I feel an urgency to put a face, literally, on the abortion discussion. Throughout these years of ministry, many others have walked these same sidewalks to offer help. We often comment that seeing the tragedy face to face impacts your perspective. You begin to understand the profound assault on the body, mind, and heart of a woman who has an abortion.

I invite you to walk with me and meet the men and women who have come to a painful crossroad in their lives. Their faces and the details of our conversations have never left my memory. They have come to an abortion clinic to solve what they consider to be a great problem in their lives. Some struggle with this decision, many don't. All will leave changed for the rest of their lives.

Integral to this ministry as a counselor is my deep communication with God. I would never have the courage or perseverance to be in front of the clinics if He were not my Constant Companion. I share my conversations with Him because I always desire that every word I speak to a client, come from His heart.

Thank you for being willing to come to the sidewalk with me today. I trust that God will open your heart to see that abortion is not an "issue". It is a heart-rending, life-altering decision that has left countless millions in our culture wounded for life.

* * *

Throughout this book, I will use "I" most of the time. Please be aware that there are over twenty people in our ministry…most of these words could be theirs, too.

To be included on our update list, where the sidewalk counselors write requests as needed, you may register your email address at thegardenofhope@gmail.com.

A Miraculous Gift

"Lord, this has been a hard morning. I'm a little uncertain about what to do with the rough-looking young man standing in the doorway of the clinic. I greeted him when he brought his girlfriend in. He had such kind eyes that I felt I could see into his soul. It unnerved me to connect that way with a stranger. But what were those eyes saying…please help us or leave us alone in this crisis? As he smokes his last cigarette before the abortion I have a final chance to touch his heart. But not without Your help, Father. Give me courage as I try one last time to discern how I can help."

"How are things going in there with your girlfriend?" I timidly began. "We have so many wonderful places that could help you both. Are you really sure about your decision to abort today?" With fear in my heart, I walked closer to the young man who eyed me cautiously. As he continued to slowly draw on his cigarette, I could get a better look at him. He was a nice-looking guy, probably in his early twenties, with dark hair. But his facial piercings gave me a little pause! He actually seemed to want to talk to me….always a good sign. We began by talking about general things, where they lived, his job, and his relationship with his girlfriend. But soon we went deeper as he assured me that contrary to what it looked like both he and his girlfriend wanted this baby.

That revelation surprised me a bit at first but I believed every word he said. He seemed eager to let me know that he really loved kids. Financial strain was the only reason they had come to the clinic to abort their baby today. His girlfriend had two other kids from another relationship. With growing panic I realized that time was moving by quickly. With increasing urgency I explained to him that just minutes from the door of the clinic was a crisis pregnancy center that would do just about anything to help them. I let him know that they helped young couples all the time and were prepared to give them information about agencies that are designed to lend a hand. By now I could see a genuine softness in this man's character. I told him he owed it to himself to at least see his little baby through an ultra-sound image. Of course, the best place for that would be the pregnancy center I had just told him about! I could see his indecision, but also his longing to keep his first child.

"This is it, Lord. You have given me the discernment to realize that behind the tough exterior that almost made me steer clear of this man, is a man of integrity. Within minutes the doctor will begin his girlfriend's abortion. As I challenge him to try one more time to convince her that there is still time to save this baby, please give this man courage. May all the softness I saw in his eyes when we first met speak volumes to this woman who holds the life of his firstborn in her hands. Somewhere inside this dark place give them a private moment in which to say what is really on their hearts. O, Lord, I am depending on You alone."

Trying to stay calm I tried one more time to assure him that all was not lost. I gently, but firmly suggested that it was "now or never". Time was of the essence. I explained how many women, even at this late moment in the decision to abort, wished that their husband or boyfriend would come into the clinic and rescue them. He seemed thoughtful about that. And then the moment I both dread and welcome, he entered the clinic for the final time. As the door closed behind him, I had no way of knowing what was about to unfold!

Within minutes the door of the clinic opened and both of them emerged. The thrill of that scene never diminishes for me! I searched the young woman's face to try to determine how she was feeling. Thankfully, she appeared to be greatly relieved! She smiled for the first time all morning and told me that they were ready to go to the pregnancy center with me to get an ultra-sound. Then, very sweetly, she asked me if I would like to see the pictures of her other son and daughter…the true heart of a mother! Within minutes this hesitant but now determined couple were being introduced to the counselors at our love-filled pregnancy center. I left them for what I thought would be a routine visit in a setting that held promise and hope. I returned to the sidewalk in front of the clinic with a smile on my face and peace in my heart. Little did I know that what was about to unfold would be some of the most dramatic events in my years on the sidewalk!

"O Lord, thank you for putting in this man a sensitive and courageous spirit. Thank you, Holy Spirit, for letting me know what would motivate him to rescue his girlfriend and baby. Thank you for this marvelous pregnancy center that always stands ready to help, and is faithful in keeping promises. Please connect this special couple with just the right counselor. Give her peace as she unravels their story. And give her great wisdom as she knits together a plan that they can accept with joy!"

Before the day was over, I was contacted by the center to ask me to enlist prayer warriors on behalf on this dear couple. Within seconds of observing the ultra-sound, the technician knew that there was a serious problem. She suspected spina-bifoda. To confirm her fears, she immediately contacted a specialist in one of the finest hospitals in our city. This committed doctor dropped everything to come and lend his expert advice. He confirmed her fears. Together they faced the young couple. They spoke honestly, read Scripture together, and outlined a plan. A promise was given that all pre-natal care would be free. And then as only God can do, the promise was also given to do the surgery on the spine absolutely free!

What a moment that must have been in that room. Just a short time before, three blocks from where they were now sitting, this desperate couple was prepared to abort their child. Now they were given the news that the baby could indeed be very handicapped. But suddenly, new information! From the lips of the tender-hearted young father the revelation that his precious twin brother had been a quadriplegic from birth due to spina-bifoda. Not only did he love him dearly, he had been involved in his constant care. How natural for him to now slip that mantle of protection on to the tiny shoulders of his first-born son. What I had seen in those deep eyes earlier in the day was the knowledge that life could be very hard, but also that love and compassion could go very far in touching the pain. Once again, God had gone ahead in this difficult place.

"Tender loving God, once again I saw something of You today. I saw You in the lives of a young couple that understood the precious gift of life, any life. I saw You in a father that is willing to do anything to protect and nurture

his child. I saw You in humble volunteers that were willing to speak the truth in love, and then offer unbreakable promises to soothe the hard places in life that shake us to the core. Today was another glimpse of Your sovereignty. Always in control of everything, even of the tiniest spine of a child not yet known to anyone but You. So to that Sovereignty, to that love-soaked, compassion-driven Sovereignty, I surrender my life once again. After what I saw today, any other choice would be folly. I love You, Father!"

I WILL ALWAYS REMEMBER THIS DAY: Months later I was invited to come to the neo-natal unit of our local hospital to visit the newborn son of this brave couple. He did indeed have a small opening in his spine. But the doctors were very optimistic about a good outcome after surgery. I was touched by his sweet beauty. He really was one of the most lovely babies I had ever seen! His proud new daddy introduced me to grandma and great-grandma. There were hugs all around. Later he and I walked out to the parking area. We laughed together as I confessed that he looked just a little scary to me on our initial meeting! Then he told me that he had come outside to smoke in those last minutes before the abortion for just one reason. He was hopeful that I could help. As we said good-bye, it struck me that the hospital is just up the hill from the abortion clinic. You can see one from the other. A place of death, a place of life. A place of despair, a place of hope. Tonight a tiny infant lay in a warm isolette. The apple of his father's eye. Forever a symbol to me of rescue and redemption gladly paid for from the treasure trove of love.

Our Faithful God

"Father, as my eyes open from sleep this morning, I realize it is 'clinic day'. It's such a busy time for me Lord. I just want to get a few things done before I go. But as I make that list, I know in my heart that time with you is more important than a perfectly cleaned house and a gourmet meal. You've asked me to do battle for You today….and time spent with You is the only way to adequately prepare. I so often settle for good, when best is available through fellowship with You. Help me prioritize, Lord."

Within minutes of that prayer I was settled in a chair, with my Bible opened on my lap. I turned the clock on the table so I could not see it. These remaining moments before my shift at the clinic had to be focused on God. He knew precisely when I needed to arrive on the sidewalk. He would get me there at the perfect time. I recognized the fact that any day in front of the abortion clinic was a day filled with unknowns. Who would the clients be? What would their needs be? How could I best show them Jesus' love? As only He can, God led me to the perfect passage….Psalm 10. What appropriate words!

'In his arrogance the wicked man hunts down the weak….he lies in wait near the villages; from ambush he murders the innocent… 'Arise, Lord! Lift up your hand, O God. Do not forget the helpless…the victim commits himself to You; You are the Helper of the fatherless….You hear O Lord, the desire of the afflicted; You encourage them and You listen to their cry, defending the fatherless and the oppressed, in order that man, who is of the earth, may terrify no more.'

My time to arrive at the abortion clinic was 10:30 AM. Precisely that time! I never liked to be late for when the clients drove through the driveway. As I drove the familiar road to my destination, I purposely avoided looking at the clock in the car. My schedule that day was in God's hands. As I approached the clinic I finally let myself glance at the clock…I was late! Three minutes late! Before I even parked the car, my partner approached me and said "See the one car in the lot? As the couple got out of their car, the man went in the clinic and the woman ran down to me on the sidewalk. In great distress she said that she was here against her will! Her boyfriend has actually held her hostage for days. She asked if we could help her escape!" My mind just froze. What was this all about? And the morning had just begun!

Before I even parked, a nurse appeared from behind the building. On her arm was the desperate client. She motioned me to come on to the property. After many years of being a perfectly 'legal' sidewalk counselor, this didn't seem right. Me? Trespassing?! But she was insistent, so I slowly made my approach on to the parking lot. Suddenly I realized something very important. If I had been on time, which would have been my way of planning things, the client's boyfriend would have seen two sidewalk counselors. Now as I boldly made my way to the frightened woman's side I appeared to be just another client. Nothing I did was suspicious to the angry man inside. As I watched the woman get into my vehicle and immediately sink to the floor to keep from being seen by her boyfriend, I knew we were involved in something very important.

"Father, I'm beginning to get the picture that this is a significant moment in time. Only You know what is ahead. This is much bigger than we could possibly be prepared for. Protect us from danger, Lord. Humanly speaking, we are in over our heads. Blind the eyes of the man inside until we are safely out of reach. Go with us on this journey, Lord....we depend on You for deliverance."

Within minutes this precious woman's story began to unfold. We had almost an hour ride to get her safely home, but it went very quickly. As if we were not even present, she began to rehearse the bizarre events of the last few days. She began by telling us she was an exotic dancer. Her relationship with her boyfriend was shallow at best. He became irate when she told him she was pregnant. Leaving no room for discussion, he told her that the baby must die on this Wednesday morning. For three days he had kept her under lock and key. And on this morning, they made their way silently to the clinic.

"Lord....what in the world do we say? Any minute now her boyfriend will discover that she left the clinic through the back door. The obvious culprits in the escape were...us! Protect us and give us wisdom. This rescue has all been orchestrated by You. We trust You to complete the task!"

My heart broke as the full weight of this tragedy washed over me. As I formed my thoughts to respond to her story, I noticed that she seemed very peaceful. In one of those moments too precious to ever let go, she calmly informed us that she knew God would rescue her. In her own words:

"I was raised in the church. I have always known Who God was. But I've had some rough times in life, and I was angry at Him. I blamed Him for the hard things that have happened to me. When I became an exotic dancer, I moved further and further away from Him. I knew the relationship I was involved in was wrong. I just wanted to be loved.

Last night, as I went to bed, I knew what today would mean for my baby. I knew that the abortion was scheduled and how forceful my boyfriend would be. And for the first time in a very long time, I prayed. I asked God to rescue my baby and I. I didn't know how...I didn't know who He would send...but I KNEW. I went to sleep in peace. Before we left for the clinic, I asked my Christian Grandma to pray. She told me she would alert the prayer chain in her church. God has answered all of the prayers today and He chose both of you to help out!"

I was stunned. I looked over at this dear woman and said "Do I have a Psalm for You! I believe God had me read the precious words of Psalm 10 early this morning, because He wanted You to hear them, as He rescued you and your little baby."

As we stopped in front of her Grandmother's house, a now confident woman burst out of the car. "Grandma! God rescued me! The baby is alive and I am just fine!" Within minutes we all gathered for prayer in the Bible-strewn living room of this faithful older saint. With great joy we rehearsed the events of the morning. Rarely in my Christian walk, had I experienced such a dramatic moving of God. What a privilege to be a part of that thrilling day.

"What can I say, God? How can I respond to what just took place? As Job so eloquently expressed when confronted with Your greatness, I cover my mouth with my hand in speechless wonder. You took a self-absorbed middle aged woman, sat her down so she could read a personal message from You, to deliver to an exotic dancer who was being held against her will, because You are The Rescuer! You are the great I AM. You orchestrate the minute details of our lives to show Your mighty power to those that surrender the circumstances of their lives to You. Father, I adore You!"

I WILL ALWAYS REMEMBER THIS DAY: My eyes have seen the deliverance of the Lord. Riding in the car with me was a woman of such profound trust in God, that I am ashamed. Someday, I pray that God lets me see the child born of such faith.

A Prayer

Reverence

"This sidewalk looks so ordinary, doesn't it Father? Just a cement pathway. It's not very wide, certainly not colorful. But we know the truth, don't we Lord? This is our meeting place. The place where God's sufficiency meets man's inability. This common place is infused with Your Glory. So no matter what I am about to face here in front of the clinic, we will walk together and face it. Back and forth, back and forth. To most people it would look tedious, perhaps even silly.

How many times haven't I come here in awe, knowing I stand on Holy Ground? This is the place where I see God at work. This is the place where I am given words of hope and wisdom that are not my own. Here is where I see You rescue Your dear creation. This simple sidewalk, more than any other location in this city, has become the place I run to, to find You.

And You never fail me. People and circumstances may fail me. My own inadequacies and lack of faith certainly hold me back. But not You. Never once have I been alone in this dreadful place. And oh, how important that is to me because I am keenly aware that 'I struggle not against flesh and blood'. I let this crack between the sidewalk and the parking lot of the clinic, serve as a reminder of the two kingdoms: Your's and satan's. The people on the other side of this line are not his, but the work that they do is most definitely evil.

As that wonderful song states, 'I stand , I stand in awe of You'. My Friend, my Helper, my Guide, my Protector. You allow Your unworthy children to witness miracles. Amazingly, You allow them to participate in Your good work. The Infinite One walks side by side with mortal man to enable and bless.

I kneel in obedience to You, Lord. This place where we meet always reminds me that I need Your divine intervention. It is a good thing that I tremble here. Holy ground and a haughty spirit don't mix. The only possible way to be affective in this dark place, is to recognize that in the words of Jeremiah: "Ah, Sovereign Lord, I am but a child!"

A Prayer

Peace

"It's amazing, Lord, truly amazing! It has been a chaotic and unnerving morning, and yet I am at peace. An awful scene has unfolded this morning. Twelve women are waiting to have their abortions. I have attempted to talk to every one of them. Some were accompanied by angry men. Others took along an obnoxious friend to run interference between me and them. The clinic staff has been angry. Many of the clients had appalling attitudes. And to top it all off the doctor gave me an evil smirk as he drove by.

What a morning! But, praise God, one of Your dearest promises: "My peace I leave with you" has been evident in every moment of this difficult day. You have not allowed me to be overwhelmed. I normally would have been… that's my personality. But You gently took hold of me and held me steady. Thank You so much! I have seen and heard so many heart-breaking things. Many of the people I spoke with were agitated and rude. But through it all You gave me simple words of truth and hope.

As I leave here today, I know that everyone was given the opportunity to 'choose the better way'. You have given us a will, Lord. We make our own decisions that forever impact our lives. It is always a powerful reminder for my own life to witness the end result of a journey marked by disregard for Your Word. There is a path that leads to destruction. We saw it here again today, didn't we, Lord?

But in the middle of very rough seas, You calmed my internal storm. Peace is a lovely thing. Thank You for that gift today."

A Boy Becomes A Man

"Lord, today isn't the day I usually go to the clinic. It's really not my shift. There's a part of me that just wants to drive by and not stop. I'm on this end of town for a pleasant reason for once. I just need to do some everyday errands. But somehow I am always drawn to this place. Maybe I'll just park outside the clinic for a minute and pray. I've learned not to dismiss these feelings of urgency. I'm sure the clients are all inside the building by now anyway. This shouldn't take long."

I had just arrived when I saw a car drive in to the parking lot. It had been so busy here yesterday on my shift, that I had forgotten what the clients' cars looked like. But this one driving in looked so familiar. I decided to get out of my car and approach the young man sitting inside. As soon as he saw me he jumped out of the car and said how glad he was to see me. That startled me but I remembered him from yesterday. Strange, I was the enemy then. Why the change? Immediately I feared the worse. What if something awful had happened to his girlfriend during her abortion?

"Father....what are the circumstances here? How do I approach this unusual situation? I know this couple was here on my shift yesterday. Why is he so eager to talk to me now? You know, Lord, that I wasn't even supposed to be here today. I've never been here on this day. Very soon I will know the significance of Your leading me to come. Please guide my thoughts, reactions, words, and responses. I am totally in the dark as to how to proceed."

The very next words out of this young man's mouth were an invitation to join him in his car to talk. He seemed desperate to have someone that would listen to him. But his car was in the clinic parking lot. And that was definitely a "No Trespassing Zone". Suddenly the thought came to me that his vehicle was his own private property. I could not be violating any law if I was a guest of the owner! Hesitantly I approached the car and reached for the door handle.

"What am I about to face, Lord? This man seems dear but is clearly agitated right now. Why is his girlfriend in the clinic without him? What if the nurses look out the window and see me in this car? I am so uneasy with all of this.... and yet, I know you will protect me. I need Your wisdom again, Father...I always do!"

I couldn't believe the tragic tale that spilled from this man's lips. Yes, they had come for an abortion yesterday. But his girlfriend was so far along, that she had to have the two-day procedure. Laminaria, small seaweed rods, were placed in her cervix. They begin to swell, causing the cervix to open so that the next day the doctor has an easier time removing the baby. But during the night, an amazing change took place in the hearts of these two young people. After they returned home from the clinic they began to have serious second thoughts about taking their child's life. Some time later they knew that they desperately wanted to save their baby.

"I can't believe what I'm hearing, Lord. You know I'm not a medical expert. If the abortion began already yesterday, I am sure that this woman is in grave danger of getting an infection if she tries to reverse things now. Is there any possible way the baby could have survived this onslaught into its safe haven? Oh, Father....You have such a perfect design for pregnancy and childbirth. There has been an enormous attack on the process. You are God over all. You are the God of the impossible. Calm my fears Lord as I listen to this man's broken heart."

Once the decision was made to discontinue the abortion, this brave young man had called the clinic to ask how they could reverse what had already begun. The clinic refused to help and said that they better get to a hospital right away to get the laminaria removed. So for the next few hours, this desperate couple went to two different hospitals to get medical attention.

Both refused to help them. Finally, a compassionate nurse made a call to the abortion clinic, insisting that they must do follow-up care on their client.

In his extreme frustration, this mild-mannered man sitting next to me said that he had gotten a little violent at the last hospital. When the doctor would not treat his girlfriend and baby, he yelled at him and overturned some equipment. The report of a disturbance was passed on to the clinic, so now he was barred from going inside for any reason. But in God's great provision, He sent me with words of comfort, help, and direction. As we sat together in a camaraderie of purpose, I began to realize the enormity of the situation.

"I think I understand, Lord. This day for errands wasn't that at all! You wanted to get me on this end of town, so I would be near to the clinic. Then You whispered to me that a little time for prayer would be a good thing. Through Your Presence, You wanted me to be a source of strength for this hurting young man. He is panicked about the welfare of his girlfriend and baby. He is exhausted and at his wits end. I should pray with him now, Lord. We'll come before the throne together."

"Would you mind if I prayed for this whole situation?" I gently began. "I know about the statistics. I know that the chance of your baby surviving this procedure is minimal at best. But I believe in a God Who does the impossible. Today He brought a housewife with a hundred other things on her mind, to this place at this time. Just to help you. Just to let you know that He saw your desperate attempts last night to reverse a decision that meant certain death for your baby." He softly answered that he would appreciate very much a time of prayer.

As soon as we finished, the clinic door opened. Out rushed his dear girlfriend. She saw me immediately. Written all over her face were the thoughts, "I shouldn't have done it! I should never have come here yesterday and started the procedure! This whole thing has been a nightmare. I should have listened to you. I am so afraid!" Without hesitation I met her outside the car door and embraced her as she began to cry. I tried to soothe her with the words that there was still a possibility that the baby could survive. I reassured her that we would do what we could to help. As she sadly got into the car, my heart broke with the realization that a baby that just yesterday was clearly dispensable, had now become the most important person in the world.

"Father, last night a boy became a man. Just twenty-four hours ago 'self' ruled this couples' thinking and decisions. They came to the abortion clinic to get rid of a baby they considered an intrusion into their lifestyle. But Someone got a hold of this young man in the night. A boy who lived for self, became a man who lived for others. A boy who lived to be the center of attention, suddenly woke-up and saw the center of his world in mortal danger. And he responded, Lord. Boldly and at great personal risk he fought for those he loves. Please honor that, Father! As I lay my hand on my shoulder where I still feel the wetness of the tears of this fragile woman, I pray a benediction on them both....Grace to you and peace from God our Father and the Lord Jesus Christ."

I WILL ALWAYS REMEMBER THIS DAY: I never think of this couple without remembering the phrase 'The cruelty of man to man." I am haunted by the scene of that night when they went from one medical facility to another, frantically seeking help. How could anyone turn them away? It was so apparent that they regretted their abortion decision. They were forced to learn the tragic lesson that abortions are not in the 'medically reversible' category. A successful abortion is a dead baby. I have often wondered if God in His great mercy spared the life of a fragile little one, whose parents recognized how precious he was, perhaps too late.

A Prayer

Discouragement

"It's too much, Lord, it's just too much. I can't come to the clinic another day! No one else cares, I am alone. The clients don't listen. The staff is rude. The Doctor mocks my feeble efforts. Evil flourishes. Children die. I try to serve You here. I long for each child's life. I hope against all hope that a mother will change her mind. I am kind when my heart says speak wrath on this hideous sin. I give a soft answer when my mouth has a hundred harsh words at the ready. I plead, I love, I show the way of life. And nobody listens!

It's quite the opposite, Lord. I am a laughing stock here. "Go home and bake cookies! Who are you to tell me what to do? How ignorant can you be with your pro-life ideas? Don't you realize this is America and we have a right to choose? Do you plan to raise this baby....if not, you have no right to talk to me. Take your judgmental attitudes and go home!"

I am tired, Father, just plain tired. With all my heart I wanted to be faithful to the end. But today I am wondering how. But that's why I'm talking to You, dear Lord. How must You feel as You literally view sin world-wide? All You asked of me today was to try. To stand. To be faithful. To care about the things that are close to Your heart. I did do that. It doesn't seem like much. But if it honors You, please accept my meager offering.

And dear Father? With Your help, I'll be back. Just never ever leave me, never let me go! I love You so much."

Gentle Spirit

"Father, it's so cold this morning. The darkness still covers the promise of morning. I feel very lonely today. I never get used to laboring alone in this call. I could use a Friend, Lord. I know You want to be that for me. Please help me be a willing servant no matter what I'm about to face."

As I approached the clinic early one dreary November morning, it was still dark outside. Immediately I realized that this was a good thing. The nurses that normally watched my every move from the recovery room windows would not be able to detect my presence. Seeing a car already in the parking lot, I was glad I could counsel without being noticed. I was surprised to see a woman alone. Slowly I got out of my car and carefully approached hers. As soon as she saw me she opened her door and came out. My heart sank. Everything about her demeanor and dress let me know that she was not a "typical client". She was soft-spoken and shy. When I saw her long skirt and straight long hair a chill ran through me. She appeared to be a Mennonite.

"May I help you in any way?" I asked. Softly she replied that she wasn't sure. "Are you here alone?" She answered that she was, her husband was at home. "Would you be willing to speak with me? I am sure that in some way I could help." She wouldn't look at me and just stared at the ground. I still had an hour to stall before the crisis pregnancy center across the street would be open to see clients. They always had just the right words to say to someone in a difficult situation. I was desperate to rescue this gentle spirit.

"Father…please help me right now. What do I say to this dear, fragile girl? Give me wisdom, Father. I need to get her out of the clinic parking lot. It's almost daylight and if the nurses discover her she will immediately be ushered inside. Give me compassion but boldness too!"

"Would you be willing to just park your car out here on the street? Then we could talk without interruption." She almost seemed relieved that I was there to talk to. Within a minute or two she was safely parked on the street and came out of her car with a very sad face and her head hanging down. As soon as she began to speak, I was touched by her story.

She was indeed a Mennonite. She had driven over an hour to get to the clinic. She was a young bride whose husband was very thrilled about the baby. This little one would be the first grandchild on both sides. But she was afraid of the future. How could they afford the baby? She just had a new job, would she lose it? What about insurance? I realized that her decision to abort was based completely on finances. At that point, I knew we had to talk, but somewhere away from the clinic. I heard myself say "Would you mind getting a cup of coffee with me?"

"Father! Why did I say that? She said yes…now what do I do with her? Where do I take her for a whole hour? I've never done this before…this can't be part of my job description, Lord! Please give me wisdom. She is so dear, a child of Yours. She must be so afraid. I feel like I'm in over my head… help me feel Your presence."

For the next hour, we rode all over town. I wasn't sure WHAT to do…so I did a lot! We had coffee, did my banking, and talked and talked. What a sad story she had. It tore me apart to realize that she had been so tortured by her decision. She had gotten out of bed very early in the morning and put her clothes on to drive to the abortion clinic. Then she looked at her sleeping husband who was so unaware of the tragedy about to take place for his wife and child. She decided to put her pajamas on and get back in bed with him. As she lay there, worry engulfed her again, and she re-dressed and left on her journey. Everything in her wanted this baby. She was confused and so alone. Her actual plan was to tell her unsuspecting husband that she had suffered a miscarriage in the doctor's office!

As she finished her story, I realized that the crisis pregnancy center would now be open. Help was on the way! We parked the car and we slowly walked toward the building. I knew that once she saw the warm and inviting counseling room, all would be well! Thankfully, she did feel instantly welcomed. I knew I could trust my friends to be kind and gentle. As I crossed the street to resume my responsibilities as sidewalk counselor I prayed fervently for what was about to take place. For the agonizing minutes I waited to see her emerge, communion with God was all that was on my mind.

"Father…this is it. You know everything hangs in the balance. Give the counselor in the center great understanding. Calm the heart of this troubled young woman. Give her Your peace, your abundant, complete, and life-guiding peace. I love You for being here with me today, Lord. I cannot function out here without You. I know that she must surrender to You to have hope. Lord! The door is opening…she is smiling…she is reaching for her car door…she is leaving!"

I WILL ALWAYS REMEMBER THIS DAY: In the darkness of a cold dreary day, God rescued. He rescued a young mother from certain despair. He rescued her precious baby from certain death. He blinded the eyes of the nurses. He gave a creative plan to a scared sidewalk counselor. He provided just the right woman to counsel at the crisis pregnancy center. An unbelievable morning in the service of an Unbelievable God!

Two Seekers

"On my drive home from the clinic I am still shaking my head in disbelief. Today may have been the strangest of all mornings, Lord. Two of the participants in this morning's abortions had a keen sense that You would not be pleased with their decision.. They actually talked about their fear that You would not forgive them. They let me see inside their souls today. Please help me sort everything out."

It's always disturbing when the person accompanying the abortion-minded woman to the clinic, is not in agreement with the decision. That was the case in two instances today…and it still bothers me. One reluctant tag-along came with his girlfriend and was the baby's father. The other young man brought his sister. Both men were very distraught that they were caught in the middle. And yet both had paid for the abortions.

The first man had already been through the abortion experience years before. At a young age he had gotten a girl pregnant. He agreed with her that abortion would be best. But now, many years later, he was still unmarried and desperately wanted a child of his own. Now his second child was about to die from abortion. Although he tried to convince her to save the baby's life, his girlfriend refused to reconsider. He even located a couple that was eager to adopt this child and pay all medical expenses. He was alone, afraid, and wanting reassurance from God.

The second man who had come with his sister to the clinic, said that their home life was not good at all. He had been his sister's protector for most of her life. He too, had done his best to convince her to keep this baby. But she didn't want to not bring a baby into a bad home situation like hers. Until she was married and established, she didn't want to have children. He was upset, alone, and worried about God's reaction.

"Lord, sometimes the ride home from the clinic is tortuous. I rehearse the facts of the morning over and over again. Could I have said more? Should I have said anything differently? Did the true compassion of Christ shine through me today? I wanted to hug each of these young men today. But I know that's not usually appropriate. I was so drawn to them because they were age of my own kids. I listened to their broken hearts and told them of your love. Continue to work in their lives, Father."

The man whose girlfriend refused to listen to him, had struggled for a long time with the concept of God. He was a believer as a small child. But then he wanted to live a sinful lifestyle so he decided to deny God. Just like that.... he tried to block Him out. Lately, he began once again to seek God. He said he would talk to Him frequently...but not in his own words, in a "redemptive way." As he stood outside the abortion clinic, waiting for the procedure to be over, he very much wanted to talk about this God he had tried to live without.

The young brother was completely devastated by his involvement in something he didn't believe was right. His deep concern for his sister and her difficult life took precedent over his own belief system. He had tried to rescue her financially and emotionally. And now he felt that the baby was keeping him from that goal. As his sister lay on the table having an abortion, he plaintively explained to me that the "Bible wasn't in his veins like it was in mine". How could he know if God disapproved of what was going on? How could he know if God would forgive him?

"O Lord, what a painful time with those two young men! I remember how carefully I measured my response to each one of them. I was representing You at that moment. Difficult questions arise about our responsibility for the sins we knowingly commit, and God's law. I realize that, humanly speaking, some sins offend me more than others. Thank You, God, that You are a Judge of perfect mercy and justice."

I remember at one point both men were in my peripheral vision. Two seekers, unaware of their great similarities. Two men that were in the middle of one of the biggest mistakes of their lives. Two wanderers that had lost their way. And so I told them the truth. I looked the boyfriend in the eye and basically told him that before his head hit the pillow tonight, he needed to think of God in a 'redemptive way'. There was just one way for him to find true forgiveness. Holding God at arms length was out of the question. This could be the day of salvation.

And to the brother, the dear tortured soul, I gently challenged him that although the "Bible was not in his veins", he had undoubtedly heard of the basic Commandments. Nodding his head, he knew that the issue at hand was the sixth. As to forgiveness, the plan-it-ahead-variety, I commended him to God. It was a loving Savior that he needed to cry out to in sincere repentance. I assured him that God loved him deeply. He prepared to leave but not before commenting "Hey lady, thanks for what you do here. I wish I had a mom like you."

"What kind of world is this, Lord? How much sorrow resides in a young man to make a total stranger appear preferable to the mother he has at home? You have placed in man a deep, deep sense of You. Many among us do their best to deny their deep thirst for a relationship with You. What kind of world is this, Lord? Why do we run to what appears to be easier, even if it is dead wrong? When did we stop calling sin, sin? How despairing does a man have to be before he willing bows the knee to the God Who made him? Blessed Holy Spirit, work in the hearts of these two men this very day. Bring them to Yourself, I humbly pray."

I WILL ALWAYS REMEMBER THIS DAY: Two men hungry for God but not recognizing it. Two men brought to a place in their lives that they never envisioned. Two men breathless for assurance that the God they have spurned, loves them and forgives all sin that is bathed in repentance. Two men shedding tears because they are afraid that the stains of this one day are too deep to cleanse. I must accept the fact that on some days babies are not saved at the clinic. There will never be a day of birth for them. But on this day, a different birth is possible. Perhaps two young men will take to heart the God of the Gospel and be born to life in Him.

A Prayer

Grief

"And so it ends. Another day at the clinic. A dozen children lost to abortion. And You and I are the only ones that know right now, Father. The city hasn't stopped its activities. The Church was not here. The women came alone. But we know. For a few minutes, I need to grieve with You, Lord. Just You and I on this cold, snowy day. I want to kneel here in Your Presence just to think about each child. Shall we remember them together, and honor their little lives?

Maybe there was a sweet baby girl who would have grown up to love music. Would she have danced before you and praised Your name? Did she have a dimple, Father? How dear of You to create that precious life. How she could have blessed others!

Was there a baby boy who would have amused You with his impish little smile, Lord? Would he have become a lover of pizza, and puppies, and mud puddle-play? Was he a bright little guy with a loving heart? I'm so sorry he's gone now, Father, so very sorry. Thank You for creating Him. He could have been a delight to his family!

So many more, Lord, so many more. Girls with a sparkle and boys with a grin. All fearfully and wonderfully made by Your magnificent design. Created to bring glory to Your most worthy Name. All discarded on this snowy winter morning.

Father, No one changed their minds and chose life for their baby. I tried my best, I really did. But today, we can't rejoice together in a saved life. So I bring to You my greatest sympathy. I mourn with You this unspeakable loss. And even in my grief, I praise You now for the marvelous gift of new life. But oh, how I wish it were more!

I'll come back next week, Lord, I promise. This despair I feel, this utter longing for things to have gone differently will not keep me away. My experience of this morning is so common to You. Grace and hope extended. Grace and hope refused. I am honored to share Your sorrow today. I will always carry in my heart Your dear precious babies. Until I meet them face to face in Heaven, I know they are safe in the arms of Jesus."

A Prayer

Comfort

"Thank you, Father for this week's sermon at church. I needed it so! That wonderful passage in Isaiah when the great prophet saw You high and lifted up. I love to think about your majesty and holiness when I stand in front of the clinic. It's imperative that I remember it here. It can be so lonely. What a great comfort to reflect on Your Presence.

'I saw the Lord, high and lifted up. And the train of His robe filled the temple with glory....and the angels cried 'Holy, Holy, Holy!!'

As I try to picture the early temple, it seems like that parking lot across the street is about the right size. Father, when I am afraid, when I am alone, I will visualize that unbelievable scene that Isaiah saw. I will visualize all that glory in these surroundings so marred by the sins of our culture. What joy to think of Your regal train of royal fabric filling this mundane place. And that's just the train. It's attached to the Kingly robe. And it belongs to You, my Lovely Lord. Your throne is high above the Heavens. But you are here, with me. You are here. Another day at his dreaded clinic. Another day of fear and reproach. But ah, Holy Father, another day in Your Matchless Presence. You are Immanuel, God with us. You are my comfort and strength. From this day on...I will 'see' Your magnificent throne room and I will know that I am safe and protected because You are my God. I love You, Father!"

Deception

"Father, there is something unusual about this couple. As they wait for their abortion they have come out of the clinic doors so often. Why aren't they waiting inside as most clients do? Please give me wisdom for this particular circumstance."

The handsome, clean-cut couple whispered together as I approached them. He was tall and blonde and looked very subdued. Her dark hair was pulled back in a pony-tail and she looked young enough to still be in high school. They seemed emotionally close, which is not often the case. He was being very sweet and attentive to his girlfriend.

"It's so unnerving, Lord, to see a couple apparently so much in love, so connected to each other. I can't help but think that they have so much going for themselves. So many of the people I see enter the doors of this clinic are hard and distant. Many couples seem to have almost no attachment to each other, they're virtual strangers. Please help these dear young people sense my concern and genuine desire to help them on this difficult day."

I was so relieved that they were willing to talk. I began by offering to be a listening ear. I could see that they were struggling with being here today. If it's possible, I like to ask a couple if they have shared the details of their situation with anyone else. So I asked them if they had a pastor or priest to talk to. The girl said she was a Catholic, the boy had no church affiliation at all. Then I asked if they had told their parents. A strange look passed between them. As I waited for them to respond, I wondered what awful family dynamics would be shared with me. Nothing could have prepared me for the news I was about to hear.

"Lord, something is wrong here. I don't think anyone but this couple knows what they are about to do. Why couldn't this young woman go to her mother in her desperate situation? Why did a knowing look just pass between them? Prepare my heart to say the right things that bring them hope and courage. If what I'm about to hear shocks me, don't let it show."

Suddenly the couple entered the clinic and I was left to try to figure out what to say next if I had the opportunity. Within minutes I did. The sober young man came out and wanted to talk. He explained that there was a reason that his girlfriend could never tell her mother about being pregnant. All her life she had been warned "not to get in the situation I was in when I was pregnant for you". As a seventeen-year-old girl, her mother had become pregnant with her. She had always regretted having a baby at a young age. From as early as she could remember, his girlfriend was terrified that she would disappoint her mother.

But the worst was yet to come. Because they lived over an hour away from the clinic, they had to be up very early to arrive on time for their appointment. Before dawn this young man had entered his girlfriend's house. In the minutes he waited for her to get ready, he noticed a note from her mother on the counter. Without saying why, the mother explained she was on her way to our city to do an "errand". It seemed very strange that she would be leaving so early in the morning, before the stores even opened. Then as they approached the abortion clinic, they were sickened to find her car parked outside. Cautiously they went inside. Within minutes they discovered the mother in the waiting room. Immediately they knew. She was there to get an abortion too.

"Lord! What kind of world is this?! My mind can't take it in! An eighteen-year-old-girl and her thirty-seven-year-old mother having an abortion on the same day! A young girl is so fearful of disappointing her mother with the news of her pregnancy that she chooses abortion. When she arrives for her dreaded appointment, her mother has preceded her in her own cover-up. Now they have spent the morning hiding from each other inside the clinic. God have mercy on them both."

For the next few minutes we pleaded with this tortured young man to try to talk with his girlfriend. We explained that he needed to be very clear with her about his deep sadness in losing his firstborn to abortion. Twice he attempted to make contact with her. First the staff, probably sensing his indecision, refused to let him see her. Then as we prayed for him, he had the courage to try again. Still trying to avoid discovery by the mother, they stole a few more minutes of talking but to no avail. He came out of the clinic looking very dejected.

Finally we accepted the inevitability of the abortion. Instead of talking on the sidewalk, we invited him into the warmth of our Prayer Room right next door. He sat there stunned. He said he had never seen this side of his girlfriend. She was so determined and rude. There was no more room for discussion. As badly as he wanted to keep this baby, it was all over. His girlfriend had all the power in the abortion decision, and she planned to use it. My heart broke as I realized that not only would he lose his baby today, it was quite predictable that soon their relationship would end as well.

I WILL ALWAYS REMEMBER THIS DAY: I often visit the city where this couple lives. I asked the young man if it would be all right if I visited him someday. Early one morning, soon after the abortion, I visited the shop where he told me he worked. We had just a minute to be alone. I asked him how he was doing, and how his girlfriend was. The story of these last hard days of his life were plainly written on his sad face. I handed him my phone number and told him I was always available to talk.

Every once in a while I drive past his shop. I still pray for him. I think of the young woman too. On a cold spring day she lost both a sibling and a child. On that same day, her mother lost a grandchild and probably the last baby she would ever have. My heart is chilled as I think of the silent sorrow in their house the night of the abortions. Two women trying to "hide their mistake" from each other chose a tortured path. Two wombs that held such promise just hours before were now empty. Two tiny members of one family were lost within minutes of each other. The generational legacy of abortion was passed from mother to daughter on the same morning in the same building. It is only a matter of time before the truth comes out. What unmatched misery and pain that day will bring.

Travail

"It's been too long, Father. I have been coming to the sidewalk at this clinic for nine months now. Nine months with no one changing their minds! Nine months of rejection. Nine months of longing and trying and hoping. As I drive the twenty minutes from my home, I am pretty overwhelmed. I know what I am about to face. And I just don't have it in me today. So, Lord, it's all You. I am totally emptied of human resolve and good intentions. And of course I know, this is just where You want me. Weak, uncertain, incapable of 'doing any good thing' on my own. Help me, Lord!"

"Good morning…could I give you some information that might be helpful to you as you wait for your appointment this morning?" I looked at this dear couple as they approached the clinic. They tugged at my heart immediately. She was a lovely Asian girl, he a young man not much taller than the young woman he held hands with as they walked closer to the door. Soft and gentle were words that came to mind. They were obviously in love and were very tender with each other. They stopped to talk just briefly but, gratefully, took the important information as they entered the clinic. I promised them that I would be outside praying, and waiting to give them more assistance.

"Lord…what a sweet couple! They seem so young and uncertain of this choice. Rarely is a man so protective of the woman he brings to the clinic. So often they display a determined attitude that 'This will get done today!' Please use the information packet to show them the truth about what they are about to become involved in. Father, I boldly pray that You uncloak satan in this place of death. He is clever at disguising himself as kind and helpful. He effectively uses the crass desires of the human soul to entice us to put self above all other considerations. He is the master of confusion and deceit. Help this young man and woman see the truth before it is too late."

Within minutes this man bolted out of the clinic door! I couldn't imagine what made him leave the building in such a hurry! And then, as though he needed to sit down or he'd faint, he collapsed on the sidewalk looking very weak. He explained that just being in the clinic made him feel physically sick. And then, with great sadness, he opened the brochure I had given him earlier and asked if the doctor would really perform one of the procedures described. I let him know that everything he read was true. As difficult as it might be to accept, the doctor options were limited in medically ending his baby's life. I gently explained that both his baby and his girlfriend were in physical danger.

He began to pour out his heart to me. He loved his girlfriend so much. Her parents were not happy with their relationship. They had wanted her to get a college education before marriage. The love I had seen between them earlier was a true portrayal of their feelings for each other. Earlier in the week, they had visited the office of the local Planned Parenthood Clinic and were told that the fetus was only the "size of a piece of rice". Although they wanted their baby, because of family pressure it just seemed easier to get rid of something so small. My mind raced as I realized that God was giving me another opportunity to expose the lies of satan. Together we determined that his girlfriend was in her thirteenth week of pregnancy. I showed him a fetal model of an eleven week preborn baby. We talked at length about the wonderful characteristics of his developing child. He was shocked and distraught.

"O Lord….help me here. These young people are so confused. They have obviously been deceived by Planned Parenthood. Help him believe and trust me. Thank you for his open heart. Thank you for this wonderful literature that is so lovingly and clearly written. And now Lord as I challenge Him to get his girlfriend out of the clinic, give him a responsive heart."

"I'm going to ask you to do something that will be very difficult for you to do. I want to challenge you to go back in the clinic and rescue your girlfriend and baby". He just stared at me. "You can do this", I assured him. "Then we can go together to a center very close to here and have a free ultra sound done. Then you can see your baby on the screen." That was all it took! What a transformation! He bounded off the sidewalk, pulled himself up to his full height of 5'5", and marched into the abortion clinic! Within minutes he emerged with his girlfriend on his arm! Though shaken by the events of the last hour, their resolve and joy were evident. Suddenly we were fast friends, bound together in the common desire to take the next positive step. I couldn't help but smile as I declared to this young man, that standing before me was one of the manliest men I had met in a long time!

Minutes later this loving couple were ushered into the safe embrace of a crisis pregnancy center. I knew that I left them in good hands as I returned to the sidewalk. They would graciously be given loving counsel, truthful words, and a guided tour via ultrasound of the wonder of God's tiny creation! I wish I could have been in that room when this brave couple saw for the first time the little life they came so close to losing. Later that day I learned that the young man was overwhelmed when he saw his baby on the screen. Immediately they knew that abortion was out of the question. With the image of their precious little one fresh in their minds, they were ready to face their parents and tell them the truth.

"Ah, Lord, You knew it all the time didn't You? You knew what this day would bring. As I drive home on the same road I traveled to come to the clinic, I am in awe of what You let me be a part of this morning. You did it all...You used every word and circumstance to rescue and save. Just hours ago, I was so discouraged. On this very road I declared that nine months was too long to travail with no results. But in Your lavish mercy, You allowed this 'turn-around' to be on the same schedule as pregnancy and birth. Nine months of waiting but today we have a baby!! How can I ever thank You, Lord? The symbolism is so profound. I know that You only ask me to be faithful...but some times, most times, I am just so... human! What if I had been unwilling to come today, Lord? Thank You...I love You!"

I WILL ALWAYS REMEMBER TODAY: What a thrill to discover that these young people were my neighbors! I was delighted when months later I was invited to a baby shower with a roomful of relatives all eager to welcome this soon-to-be-born little life. Not long after this special celebration, I held this precious baby in my arms. As I looked into his beautiful face, I marveled at what God had done. I still smile at his pictures that grace my home. I think of the day that his brave young father risked much but gained everything when he rescued both the woman he loved and the son she carried. To God be the glory!

A Prayer

Fear

"Father, they've called the police again. Thank you that for all these years you have protected me from the clinic's desire to intimidate me. They often attempt to make things difficult, but it never materializes. This time, they threaten, it will be different. They are pretty convinced that I'll be taken away.

Lord…I am so surprised at my reaction! I am afraid. I am debating whether or not I have the strength to go to jail. I knew this day could come. It comes for so many of Your children around the world. I always thought I would be brave and calm. I am so disappointed in myself. Give me peace!

I was told if I leave now, the police wouldn't come after me. I have just a few minutes before they arrive! With my husband out of town, what about the kids? They would be so afraid to get the news that I am in jail. Lord, this is difficult.

As I go to my knees in these final moments, I have decided to stay. You can take care of the details that bring me fear. You have always been my 'hope and stay'. I must stand with You to the end! God help me…give me the courage I could never possess on my own. You are my only comfort in life and death. You are my comfort now."

Helpless Before Almighty God

"I am excited to see if there is a difference this morning, Lord. This is the first time I have come to counsel since the opening of our place of prayer, The Upper Room. I am so glad someone challenged us to provide a place of prayer right near the clinic. What will it be like with a prayer center just a few feet from the wall of the procedure room? I love the thought that while we counsel with men and women on the street, other believers will be going before Your great throne on our behalf. Lord, please bless this new endeavor!"

It was still dark as I drove up the street to the clinic. For the first time in many months I felt a sense of expectation as I prepared to meet with the clients that were scheduled for abortions. As I parked my car I noticed some commotion on the side of the clinic building. This was very unusual. Normally people preferred to enter the building as soon as they could. There was very little standing around.

"Father, it's so dark I can't determine what is going on. What is the great confusion? Why is that young woman yelling her boyfriend's name? Am I seeing correctly? Is she holding him up? Lord, help me sort this out. Protect me from any danger. Help me as I step out into the darkness of this uncertain morning."

A great drama unfolded before me as soon as my feet made contact with the sidewalk. In the few seconds it took me to approach the couple huddled in the corner, I saw the man fall down on to the sidewalk. He fell very hard and was sprawled out on the pavement adjacent to the clinic building. His girlfriend repeatedly called out his name, but there was no response. He was motionless. He was out cold.

"What is happening here, Lord? You know I am so unequipped to handle medical emergencies! Has this man fainted or is it more serious? Should I call an ambulance or try to take him somewhere in my own vehicle? Father, I am in serious trouble here. My mind absolutely freezes up when someone is having physical problems. I must do something...please give me wisdom!"

The frantic girlfriend was saying something that at first I couldn't understand. But with great relief I finally realized that she was saying that her mother would be here soon because she was just parking the car. As we both attempted to help the young man, her mother came running up behind us shouting in fear as the seriousness of the situation dawned on her. When she had dropped the couple off, all appeared fine. Now her daughter was in a complete panic, the boyfriend had not moved a muscle, and there was no help in sight.

"Lord, You know if this young man is too fragile to move. Thank you for sending the mother back here in time. Thank you that she is driving a van so there will be enough room for the young man to lay down in the back. Please send someone to help us move him into the vehicle. I am so grateful that I am never truly alone here."

Just then I heard a weak voice say, "You know I don't want you to have this abortion. I never did." It was the young man. Although still somewhat confused, he wanted to make the point that this was not his choice for their baby. With great warmth, his girlfriend assured him that they didn't have to go through with the abortion. They could leave right then if that's what he wanted. After a few more minutes of tender interchanges between them, we felt it was time to move him into the van. I looked up from my position on the sidewalk to see another young man walk by. He was about to enter the clinic. Quickly I asked him to assist us in moving the still-weak man up off the ground.

"Lord, we're ready to go...but where? I'm so glad this all happened under cover of darkness, or the staff in the clinic could have invited him inside to recuperate. Now at least this couple can make their abortion decision in "safer territory". Go ahead of us, Father. Be on our right and left, before and behind us. I trust the outcome of this troubling morning to You."

Before we had left the area of the clinic, everyone was determined not to go to the hospital. They really felt that things were going to be all right. When I suggested they needed to talk further about their situation, they agreed. It seemed that this baby was beginning to be important to both of them. I mentioned our wonderful crisis pregnancy center. I told them what would take place there and they seemed eager to go. With out further delay, they followed me in the van as we drove to a place of certain help and promise.

As we drove the short distance to the center, my mind lingered over what I had just witnessed. An otherwise healthy young man just fell over as he came near to the abortion clinic. He was actually on the property of the apartment building next door, the location of our newly opened prayer room! It was as though he ran into an invisible wall. It was simply impossible for him to take another step closer to the clinic door. My mind tried to process what my heart understood.

"Lord!! It was You! By Your great power You have stopped the advances of the enemy, the evil one, satan. You have honored our feeble attempt to set-up a place of prayer. You melted away the strength of the man who would have been part of a travesty this morning. His little baby would have been the first one sacrificed on the altar of self since we opened the doors of the Upper Room. But You wouldn't let it happen! You have shown me that You will be my strong tower in times of trouble."

Within minutes we were all gathered in the van as we waited for the center to open. I listened intently as the couple discussed their future openly with each other. By now it was clear… there would be no abortion. The staggering events of the last hour were enough to convince them that they were dealing with a very serious matter. All three of them had seen a "STOP" sign of major significance. And now none of them had the least desire to ignore a warning so clear and bold.

I WILL ALWAYS REMEMBER THIS DAY: It doesn't matter to me if there was a simple medical explanation for what I saw. Whether or not this man fainted, had low blood sugar problems, or just was overcome with emotion because of what he was about to participate in. To me, it felt like an Old Testament moment. The Great Jehovah stops the advancing army cold, flat out cold. I was so reassured that day. I am always aware that we 'struggle not against flesh and blood but the spiritual forces of evil in the heavenly realms.' All that warfare going on that we cannot see. What's a weary Christian to do? For me it's very simple. I like to think back to an early morning when I saw with my own eyes the result of my Invisible God doing battle for me. Decisive, uncompromising, victorious! Christians arise! Your Deliverer has come!

The Hard Truth

"Father, I cannot believe what I'm about to face. I know enough about this woman's story to be in utter shock. As I sit across the table from this wounded woman, I know my heart will not be able to absorb her story. She appears so gracious and soft. Help me respond as You would. Don't let my face reflect the horror I'm certain to feel. She needs compassion, not judgment. Let nothing in my demeanor say 'We tried to warn you'! Great God of mercy, enable me to be embrace this woman and be a conduit of Your grace."

My friend and I were meeting in a bustling fast-food restaurant for lunch. The reason for our meeting was extremely unusual. A recent client of the abortion clinic where we sidewalk counsel asked for a meeting. One day, four months after her abortion, she returned to the clinic in search of a listening ear. She needed to tell someone about the nightmare she had lived through since the day she entered the clinic to abort her baby.

From her heart to ours:

"I was over 22 weeks along, not quite 23 weeks. I was given a shot of something before the abortion, I guess because I was so far along. As I entered the surgical room I was struck by the fact that none of the instruments the doctor was about to use were in sterile conditions. Everything was just laying out on a towel. I had been feeling my baby move for several weeks now, so as I got up on the table I was having second thoughts. After they prepared me for surgery, the doctor entered the room. He didn't say a word. I told him I was having doubts about aborting my baby. His only response was that I was here for an abortion, and it was too late to change my mind.

That was the last time he spoke. During the entire surgery he didn't say anything to me. When he was finished he put my baby in a steel bowl. By then I was crying and asked to see it. I felt this deep desire to see my little one. I was so sorry that I had gone through with the abortion. But the doctor just covered the bowl with a towel and silently left the room.

I was feeling miserable by this time and bleeding heavily. The nurse told me to just sit for a while and I would be fine. But the bleeding continued. It was getting to be late in the day, and I guess the staff wanted to go home. I was feeling too weak to drive, but no one in the clinic offered to give me a ride. Instead they gave me another shot that they said would reverse the first one. As I stood to leave, I began to hemorrhage. I bled through all my clothes. The nurse gave me one of those blue plastic table pads to wear on the outside of my jeans so I wouldn't ruin the seat in my car.

My home was nearly 25 minutes away on a busy highway. Somehow I made it into the door before I collapsed. The hours that followed were a nightmare. I was in such pain. My twelve year old daughter helped with my other kids, but she was getting very concerned about my condition. By the middle of the night I was in bad shape. I knew I needed to go to the hospital, but I didn't want to ride in an ambulance. Thankfully a neighbor drove me to the emergency room.

For the next eight days, I hovered between life and death. I was in a Catholic hospital and they gave me last rites. The doctors were not sure I was going to make it. The problem was that the man who had done my abortion left parts of the baby inside of me. I had developed a massive infection. I am so sorry I had this abortion."

"Lord, as these words of deep pain and remorse tumble from this woman's lips, You alone can give her comfort. She is wounded physically and emotionally. She knew before her baby was aborted that this wasn't what she truly wanted. But now, of course, her decision is irreversible. Nothing will bring her little one back. Have mercy on her tortured mind, Lord. Help us bring a measure of compassion to her broken spirit."

In the time we remained together, we did our best to enter into this woman's immense pain. Here sitting before us was a lovely woman, graciously attending her two year old. She rocked him, cuddled him, wiped his darling little face. All the while the words of a nightmare beyond understanding, spilled from her lips. Over and over again she rehearsed the events of that day. All we could do was listen and silently pray. It was all so disturbing that we were at a loss for words.

We talk about 'surreal moments'. This was one of them. Moments of pain and torture had just been described to us. A horrible, verifiable event had taken place in the life of the beautiful mother sitting before us right in my own city. As we said our good-byes I glanced around the restaurant. Everything looked so normal. Happy people having a casual lunch with friends. No one would suspect the nature of the discussion that the three of us had just shared. On an ordinary day in a small town, I heard details of a woman's abortion experience that haunt me to this day. I will never be the same.

I WILL ALWAYS REMEMBER THIS DAY: The irony of this situation is so striking. A client who at one time had been approached by sidewalk counselors and had been offered help, disregarded their counsel and chose a late-term abortion for her child. But when she nearly died from the procedure, she returned to that very sidewalk to pour out her heart in agony. Within weeks of our initial meeting we had mobilized the body of Christ to lovingly minister to this woman. Donations of help poured in. Carpet was laid in her house; furniture was delivered; groceries were supplied; and her family was presented with a beautiful Christmas tree and gifts of clothing and toys. She will always remind me of God's surprising grace. A grace so profound that in the middle of our darkest night, brought on by our own sin, He breaks through in love. He asked the community of believers to express His mercy to a wounded soul, and they did. How like Jesus to remind us through an encounter with a woman who discarded the life within her, that He came to declare a message of eternal life that is forever secure in Him.

A Plan Of Hope

"Father, I sense great anger coming from this young man. He is so hostile. Help me know what his problem is. I'm relieved to see that his attitude to his girlfriend is much different. He is caring and gentle with her. Thankfully, he really seems to love her. Now that she has entered the clinic to register, help me as I approach him. You know his needs and his concerns. I really hesitate to start with him. Nothing about him says 'Welcome'."

I addressed him as though I were confident he'd be delighted to talk with me. "What's going on with you guys today? Is there anything I can do to help?" Immediately the young man bristled. He told me that he was not very happy with 'Christians' in general, and pro-life ones in particular. It was a beautiful, warm day. I thought if we could just talk, I might be able to help him with his deep frustrations. I invited him to sit on the grass and tell me about their situation. Surprisingly he agreed to join me. He explained to me that although he and his girlfriend attended church, they were pretty certain that fellow Christians would be nothing but judgmental about their circumstances. To make matters worse, their parents supported their decision to "choose what was best."

"And now what, Lord? They have their parents O.K. To make matters worse, he doesn't like Christians and seems to distrust them. They were both raised in the church, but it's the last place they would go for support. That is so sad. Have believers disappointed him in the past? Is he correct in characterizing Christians as judgmental? Keep him talking to me, Father... and please, totally direct this conversation."

As we talked, this young man with the tough exterior began to soften. He was so mixed up. I gently asked him if he would be willing to go in and ask his girlfriend to come out and speak with me. I was hoping that she could give more insight into what brought them to the decision to abort their baby today. Although I assured him she would only hear kindness, he didn't seem eager to go and get her. But then he seemed to realize what was at stake here and suddenly he got up and hurriedly walked into the clinic. I was surprised how quickly he came out again with his girlfriend by his side. Now was the crucial time.

"I have been praying for you all morning", I told her. "I know something about your situation from your boyfriend. You must trust me that there is help available. You have so many options". She listened intently. As we stood there in the warm sun, I felt so hopeful. With her sweet personality and gentle ways, I just felt so drawn to her. I felt that I could help her personally.

Out of my mouth came words I had only said once before in all the years I sidewalk counseled. It just seemed like the right thing to do! Without weighing every possibility I just blurted out "I want to offer you my home to live in. You may come to live with our family. For the next six months, I will pay for all your care. We will take care of everything for you. I've got great kids and a wonderful dog…you'd love them! You can come over with both your parents tonight and interview us all. You can sit in our home, check it out, and be quite sure we're normal! Please, no matter what brought you to the point of wanting this abortion today, we can work it out together".

"Lord…what have I just promised? I will definitely have some explaining to do to my husband when I get home! But I want to show her Your great love in a tangible way. I know I can trust You to work out all the details. The doctor will arrive at any moment…and the abortions will begin. Please, Father….I feel so connected to this young couple. It's been almost three hours of talking, and hoping, and longing. How I want her to leave this place right now! As unusual as it would be for us as a family to have her come live with us, I know we could depend on You to see us through."

Within minutes the time I have come to dread arrived. The doctor drove into the parking lot. It was one of those moments when my surroundings seem to freeze in time. For a minute no one moved…and then I heard from her lips something I hadn't even considered. She simply announced that she would like to go in to the clinic now and have her abortion. I literally could not believe it. For hours, words and explanations were carefully laid out. Hope-filled solutions were extended and trustworthy promises given. And to her, it was not enough. She had her mind made up, discussion closed. I looked into that dear face. The one that throughout the morning I had begun to picture in my house, sitting at my table, being nurtured by my loving family. She hugged me, and politely thanked me as I began to cry. Then she disappeared behind the clinic door.

"Father, I am almost too distraught to talk. I was so sure things would have turned out differently. We could have made a home for this dear one, a safe place. My three teenagers would have loved her. With Your help, we would have been faithful to all the promises I extended to her. And so dear Lord, I join you in the sorrow You feel every minute of every day. Your precious love is extended and unfathomably spurned. How do you bear it? Time and time again, Your creation defies You. God, have mercy!"

I WILL ALWAYS REMEMBER THIS DAY: A girl so close to rescue turns her back on the offer of family, nurture, and hope. And adding to that grief I later discovered that through a shared work situation, she was already in relationship with my son and daughter. My kids had talked often of the great time they had together. It hurt even more to realize that to have included her into our family circle could have been a very special and comfortable journey. Her face still haunts me. God had given us an instant rapport on that crucial day in her life. Now I mourn what could have been and grieve that we were not able to lavish her with the love of Jesus.

The Bravest Man

"I am still reeling from the events of this morning, Lord. As I look back I realize what a phenomenal event just took place. Something so contrary to the nature of man. In spite of my great weaknesses here on the sidewalk, You allowed me to see Your great power. Thank You, Lord...I didn't deserve being in the middle of this amazing display of Your tenacious love."

It was a morning when I was eager to catch-up on the week's events with the others who had come to the clinic to pray or counsel with me. I had asked for God's help as I did for every shift. As the clients drove through the driveway to park in the clinic's lot, each one was offered help. But before long several of us were engaged in deep conversation. And then I heard it. The softest voice saying something to me I couldn't quite hear. I wasn't even sure if I heard the statement correctly. I turned to face a heart-wrenching scene.

"We'll take that help you offered us", I heard the man say. For a minute, I wasn't even sure what he was talking about! What had I said to this couple as they stopped to receive literature from me just a few minutes before? Thankfully God was in control of all the details and He firmly pulled my mind and heart back into the situation that faced me.

"O, Lord. I'm so sorry. I've been talking with my friends and not concentrating on the task before me. It's so easy for me to become distracted. It's always hard to be here and I am only too eager to let my mind escape to more pleasant conversation. Usually I have some connection to each couple after speaking to them for just a minute or two. But not now. Help me, Lord! I am totally in the dark."

As I gave my full attention to the couple standing before me, my heart was gripped as I noticed that the woman never spoke. Not one word. She just stood crying soundlessly. Her husband gave all the details, and they were so hard to listen to. This plain-looking wife and mother had an affair with someone from work. They had two older children, and her husband was unable to have any more. All their friends and relatives would know that this was not his baby.

"Father! Am I hearing this correctly? She does not look like a woman who would ever have an affair. A few weeks ago her husband probably thought that they were just a typical couple going to work and raising their kids. And now this. Give me wisdom, Lord. I have never asked a man in this situation to do what I'm about to suggest."

"Would you ever consider letting your wife continue in this pregnancy and then choose adoption for the baby?" I gently offered. With great feeling he explained that as he sat inside the abortion clinic, he knew that he could not take the life of this baby, even if it was not his. But now he was faced with a terrible dilemma. His family, friends, and perhaps even his children would know that his wife had been with another man. And to raise another man's child would be a constant reminder of his wife's unfaithfulness and almost more than he could bear. Yet with great courage, he had finally decided that he would be willing to let the pregnancy continue, and then give the baby up for adoption.

"What a brave man, Lord! Thank You for helping him make this unbelievably difficult decision. He has chosen life for this child that is not his own. He will stand by his wife, help her through this pregnancy, and be there for the birth of a child that represents the most devastating circumstance of his married life. Protect us now as we make the drive to the Christian adoption agency."

Within minutes we were on our way. I watched this couple in my rear-view mirror as they followed closely behind in their vehicle. In all my discussion with her husband on the sidewalk at the clinic, the wife still had not spoken.

And now as we drove on the highway, I could see her lowered head as she continued to weep. My spirit immediately cried out against satan. Another victim deeply wounded. He lures us into sin and we are eager to accept his claim that it will be pure pleasure with no consequences. But driving in the car behind me was a graphic reminder that sin always results in heartache.

As we entered the building and waited for the counselor that would carefully explain the adoption process, I was struck again by the integrity of this man standing in front of me. I felt it was appropriate to tell him that he was a man of great kindness and strength. I told him that few men would put aside their pride for a tiny infant, not their own. As I looked at his broken-hearted wife I reminded her that in spite of all she had done, God had blessed her with a husband of great character. For the first time in a very long morning, she responded. Without a word, she nodded her head.

I WILL ALWAYS REMEMBER THIS DAY: What an incredible price we pay for participating in a lifestyle that displeases God! A visual reminder was watching a woman so broken, so humiliated that she was virtually rendered speechless. As she realized the enormity of the pain that was inevitable for her husband, children, family, and friends, I'm sure her perspective of the affair changed dramatically. Satan tried to involve her husband, too. He whispered that it would be so simple to erase this child conceived in deception. For a few minutes a conflicted soul considered the evil one's plan and drove his wife to the abortion clinic. If he would just sacrifice this child, his pride would be intact. No one would ever know. But then, by God's grace, this brave man turned from destruction to life. And now, a vulnerable baby lies safely in its mother's womb unaware of the personal cost a noble man chose to pay.

A Prayer

Joy

"There is no feeling like this, Lord. I have felt Your Presence all morning. I have seen You work in the willing heart of a client. And now they have chosen life! All the praying, and hoping, and longing for a change of heart has happened. You have supplied my every need. You have given me wisdom to know what to say. You have given me boldness and urged me to intervene in the life of this couple.

And the joy that they feel as they leave the clinic, has spilled over into my heart. I love to see the change in their whole demeanor as they realize how close to disaster they had come. But You rescued them by Your powerful right arm! Their baby is safe from physical danger and they will be spared great emotional trauma.

I know the path before them may have some great difficulty. Everything may not go smoothly in the days ahead. But I assured them of Your blessing, help, and protection. I told them that they have honored You because they were willing to swim upstream against the current of the culture. Theirs is a world that often devalues life. It is a place where tolerance is the byword, and self the principle god.

Today a brave young couple cast their lot with You, Father….and I couldn't be happier! I rejoice with You, Lord as Your sweet creation has been deemed precious. All that satan had waged against this young life has not come to completion. The parents of this blessed baby saw hope in a time of despair. They saw You, Father…strong and mighty to save.

To You I lift a doxology of praise:
'Praise God from Whom all blessings flow Praise Him all creatures here below Praise Him above ye Heavenly hosts Praise Father, Son, and Holy Ghost.

Amen.'

A Prayer

Danger

"I was threatened again today. An irate boyfriend didn't take too kindly to me mentioning that perhaps there could be a better choice. He charged me at the sidewalk. As he was coming at me like a bull-moose, I thought of those phrases of comfort from Your Word. That You would be with me, and surround me with Your watch care. But at that moment, it was very threatening.

As he came inches from my face, his anger just dissipated. Just like that! He seemed powerless to follow through with his threat. Now why would that be, Father? Perhaps because Your Word is true? As I reflect on this incident, I realize that in all these years, no one has ever been able to lay a finger on me. Some have wanted to…but no one has been able to. Thank you Father. Never a dull moment in Your service. I love you…You definitely keep things exciting!"

Dance Of Joy

"Father, there is something very sad here. A mother and daughter just pulled in to the clinic parking lot, but the father drove separately. I've never seen that happen. He seemed eager to speak to me and assure me that he loved his daughter dearly, but he couldn't support her decision to abort her child. There is such sadness in that man's eyes! He and his wife are an older couple and I wondered if this beautiful daughter was a child of their later years. How precious she seemed to both of them! Lord, give me wisdom."

As the mother and daughter entered the clinic, the dad slowly left and went to the restaurant next door. It broke my heart to see this family separated at such a difficult time. I couldn't help but wonder about the pain they were all feeling. Had heated words been exchanged? Were tears shed on the way to the clinic this morning? Within the hour the two women came out of the building. They must have called the restaurant and asked to send the dad outside. I watched this painful drama from a distance.

Slowly the two women made their way over the grassy hill to the restaurant next to the abortion clinic. As if on cue, the long-faced father came out of the door. They met on the patio and the conversation was very intense. No one reached out for each other, their arms were held close to their bodies. From that body language the message was clear. At this point an abortion was his daughter's chosen course. Silently they parted ways. No final hugs were exchanged. As the man re-entered the restaurant to wait, his wife and daughter once more approached the clinic.

"Should I interfere at this point, Lord? There is so much I want to say to these two suffering women! It is so very clear that the dad loves his daughter, but he can't bring himself to sit by her side as she waits for her abortion. The love between them all is so obvious. How abortion affects the whole family, God!

This dark day in their lives will never be forgotten. Holy spirit give me the words to talk to them if that is Your desire."

Just as the two women walked back on to the clinic parking lot, I gently interjected "May I help you today? Are you pretty sure that this is the direction you want to go?" You could see the pain and indecision on the young woman's face. She answered that she wasn't completely sure if an abortion was the answer. Carefully I mentioned that it seemed that her dad wasn't comfortable with them being here today. I asked if I was right about that. She nodded sadly, and confirmed my suspicions. But her last words gave me hope…they assured me that they still had doubts.

"As I walk out here on the sidewalk and pray for what is going on in this family's life, I think about how the dad in the restaurant reminds me of You, Father. Is this how You feel about my rebellion? You make the right path clear, You watch as I sometimes move headlong into sin, and yet You never stop loving me. Just as this tortured father can't stand to be away from his daughter, so You wait for me. Lord, there is still time for this young woman to change her mind. It seems to be tearing her up inside to go against her dad's wishes for her life. Please remind her of their special relationship as she waits in these final minutes before her abortion. Please help me take a lesson from this. Don't ever let me ever forget that when sin crouches at my door, Your love is sufficient to help me flee and choose the better way."

Suddenly the door of the clinic opened. I couldn't believe it! There stood the mother and daughter smiling broadly. They began to get in their car, a very good sign. As they drove past me, they stopped to let me know that the young woman had decided against an abortion. I was so relieved and happy! I knew where their next stop must be! As they walked up the ramp to the restaurant, as if on cue, the dad emerged once again to greet them. What a different scene than the hour before! The young woman ran up and threw her arms around her dad's neck. For a long time they just held each other. Then they looked long into each other's faces with deep love. A celebration lunch was in order. As they went towards the restaurant they linked arms. Father and daughter united again! The joyous dad danced a little jig as he realized that both his daughter and grandchild were safe.

"Father…how can I ever thank you for letting me observe that touching scene. It was all so much like the prodigal son story in the Bible. We go out to make are own decisions, regardless if they hurt Your heart. But when we are reconciled to you, we know You have been waiting all the time! You long to embrace us. I know Your Father's heart dances with joy when we return to Your side."

I WILL ALWAYS REMEMBER THIS DAY: After a scene like that, I had the overwhelming urge to congratulate these special people! I left my post at the sidewalk to do some quick shopping. A little stuffed bear, with baby powder and lotion would be just fine. Very soon I entered the restaurant to find a happy family of three eating lunch. They smiled as I approached the table. "May I be the first to give the baby a gift?" What a privilege to share in their joy!

Arms Of Love

"Father, as I approach this car entering the clinic parking lot, I am surprised that both the man and woman are crying. To see the emotion of sadness before the abortion is so rare. Almost all hearts are saddened afterwards. This is such a unique situation. Give me wisdom, kindness, and compassion. O no, Lord. They have a little one in a car seat in the back... she looks about two years old. Please rescue this young family from the certain pain of what lies ahead."

"Good morning", I carefully began. "I'm here to help you in whatever way I can. Is there anything I can do for you this morning?" As their car slowed to a halt, I heard sniffling from the woman and saw sorrow on the man's face. They were quite young, maybe still in their teens. The vehicle they were driving told the story of hard times. I couldn't help but compliment them on the little angel in the back seat. She smiled at me so sweetly as I talked to her mom and daddy. Gently I probed for the reason for their decision to abort their second child on this day. I was not surprised to hear the details of the sad story that spilled from broken hearts. It was simple really. Although they treasured their little daughter in the back seat, they just felt too young and too poor to bring another child into the world.

"Oh, Father, how tragic this all is. I can tell from their wounded spirits that an abortion is not at all what they want. It's so frustrating that I'm just a stranger to them. How will they believe my offer of help? Help me convince them that You will provide. Help them see that if they trust You, their earthly concerns will be met. I beg You, Lord...intervene! Soften their hearts to the truth."

"If I may just make a comment...in my estimation, no one is a candidate for this procedure. But I almost never see a couple as upset as you are, before their abortion. You are certainly going to be emotionally devastated if you go through with this." Although they listened politely, even agreed, their minds seemed to be focused on getting in to the clinic. Ironically, in many ways it probably appeared to them to be a safe haven. It offered, in their minds, an end to their most immediate "problem". My mind struggled for words that would be more convincing. Nothing worked. My heart sank as they slowly pulled away from me and into the clinic parking lot. Within minutes the woman was dropped off and she walked towards the building. The last words she heard me say was that I would not leave her. I assured her that every time she looked out the waiting room window, I would be there on the sidewalk. She would be able to see me waiting for her. I was there to pray and my dearest hope was to take her safely home before she had the abortion.

"Lord…I can hardly stand this! I cannot bear it that she is in there all alone. Help me keep the vigil. Keep me faithful in the hours ahead. I will walk and pray holding on to that wonderful verse… "Against all hope, Abraham in hope believed." I need to remember his example, Father! He was such a faithful servant. When he couldn't see the road ahead, he trusted You. When life was difficult, He rested in You. He shared Your longings, held on to Your dreams. I know what you want for this woman and child, Lord…LIFE. It is not Your wish that this precious baby dies here today. I will not give up hope! Strengthen me."

As the hours ticked away, I refused to give up hope. This tender young mother was one I longed to see change her mind. As I walked back and forth on the sidewalk I imagined the joy I would feel when I saw the front door of the clinic open. I visualized her running to me and asking me to take her home to her husband and little girl. I just knew that this story would have a happy ending. As I continued to pray and long for her escape from certain agony, the abortionist suddenly drove in. I was so deeply in prayer that I had failed to realize that it was time for his arrival and for the abortions to begin. I couldn't believe this was happening! Opportunity for a changed heart was getting very short. She would have to run out of that building very soon. Surely, at any minute, I would see her run out of the clinic to safety.

"No Lord! No!! Not this one! I have longed for her and her baby's life all morning. I have prayed with great urgency. I have hoped, against all possible reason, I have hoped. O God…intervene! Save this child and its mother. What do You want me to say? Just tell me what to do and I will do it. I beg You… not this one. But I know. Father, I know about the will of man. You have allowed us the freedom to rebel against Your laws. I know that Your heart is broken right now, too. I am so sorry for this horrible place. I boldly ask, in Your great mercy, protect this woman right now. Even as she chooses death for her little one, please protect her life from the doctor's carelessness."

Time dragged on from that point. I knew that the baby was dead, but I couldn't seem to leave my place on the sidewalk to go home. Soon the clients that were finished began to return to their cars. Finally the sensitive young father came to pick-up his wife. As he opened the car door he looked my way. There was so much knowing in the glance between us at that moment, so much pain. I had an overwhelming urge to enfold this tortured couple in my arms. I gently asked him if he would tell his wife that I wanted to hug her before she went home. He nodded sadly, and went inside the clinic.

Soon they both came out the front door, and she was crying. With great tenderness I reached for her and she willingly let me hold her tightly. I rocked her like she was my little girl. Then I took her tear-stained face in my hands and assured her that at that very moment she was dearly loved by God. The look on her face was one of disbelief. Could it be? After what she had just done? Minutes ago she had paid someone to end her baby's life! As I looked into that sweet face that will never leave my memory, I could assure her that Jesus was the forgiving Savior. There was nothing He could not forgive. If she sincerely repented, He would be her True Hope. Through tears of immense grief, she thanked me and slowly entered her car to go home.

"Thank You long-suffering Savior. Thank You that You have allowed Your children the unspeakable privilege of being Your arms of love to a hurting world. Thank You that in a moment too tender to articulate, I was able to hold a fellow human being so close to despair, and offer hope in Jesus.

Dearest Father, I pray that as I rocked this precious young woman, still bleeding from her abortion, she could only feel Your arms, and hear Your great offer of forgiveness. Go with this couple, Lord. Protect them from satan's inevitable advances on their souls. May the dread experience of this day, through the wonder of Your grace, bring them to the feet of the cross where they may find mercy and redemption."

I WILL ALWAYS REMEMBER THIS DAY: Incredibly, shortly after this horrendous day, the abortion clinic closed for good. For years people had been praying that this place would close down. In God's mercy, it went out of business. But not before God burned in my memory the face of one more precious woman. One who taught me that although my heart is moved to save babies, it must be equally intense about their mothers. And not just the mothers who choose life. Jesus passionately proclaimed the message that He came for the sin-sick. His message was the outstretched arms of love. I must do no less.

The Dancer

"Oh Father, I need help now! This young woman's car is not in very good shape…but I don't want to offend her by asking if she needs financial help. It's so obvious that she isn't wealthy. Lead me to say the right thing. I depend on You for every word, every observation I make with so little information. I want to help her, Lord! Here goes…."

Slowly the sweet young woman started to get out of her car. She seemed so thoughtful, or was it just plain reluctance to follow through on her decision to come to the clinic in the first place? "Good morning! I'm just here this morning to offer what help I can. May I ask if you are here for financial reasons?" Tall and slender, honey-brown hair pulled tightly on top of her head. She looked like a ballerina. Softly she answered "That's the only reason I'm here!" Reassured that I had observed correctly I ventured further, "You won't believe the number of people I can get to help you!" With that said, I gained further boldness "Why don't you come over here by our parking lot? We'll be able to talk so much better!" Miraculously she entered her car again and headed to our lot. Within a minute or two she would be right in front of me, waiting to hear in what way I could help her. Adrenaline pumped through me as I realized that the next few minutes could be a life or death matter.

"Father!! She's on her way. You know how clutched I become when a client is actually willing to listen. I am so used to getting rejected that when they DO come over to talk, I barely know in what order to explain so much information. Does she need to hear about the baby's development? Has she ever been pregnant before? What will grab her heart the most? What is her greatest need? Help me remember all the resources available. Father…help me be loving and compassionate no matter what I'm about to hear about her life and circumstances. You have called me to "be Jesus" here, but I'm so human. Only with Your amazing Presence will True Hope flow through me. Here she comes!"

I approached the young woman's car and got a better look. I always look for a wedding band or engagement ring on a client's finger, but there wasn't one. And there in the back seat I saw that she had a little toddler with her. I noticed he wasn't in a car seat. It didn't dawn on me at the time that maybe she couldn't afford one. She rolled down her window and I smiled my brightest smile. "I'm so glad you came over by me, we can help in so many ways! Do you have other kids at home?" She told me at that point that she had two in school…and the little guy in the back seat. Then I heard a sentence I don't hear very often. "If I don't have this abortion I will lose my job!" I countered "Really? Most places can be very understanding." My mind was going 90 miles an hour…what kind of job would fire you for being pregnant?! McDonalds wouldn't care, nor would a secretary job be a problem. Maybe she was just scared about telling her boss. Carefully I asked "What kind of work do you do?"

"O Lord, there seems to be a big problem here! Some heartless boss would actually fire this dear girl for being pregnant. She's so sweet and gentle. Life obviously has been very hard for her. It seems that she has no husband and already has three kids to raise alone. No wonder this pregnancy seems like the last straw. If she is struggling to make ends meet I'm sure the prospect of one more mouth to feed could throw her into despair. Wisdom, Lord! I need Your wisdom."

"Well she slowly started to explain, I'm a dancer." (Were my instincts right that she looked as lovely as a graceful ballerina?) "You know…an exotic dancer at an Adult Club". (Ahhh, no. That I wouldn't know much about!) Suddenly my mind kicked in gear. In her mind at this moment, she had everything to lose if she stayed pregnant. Her job was the means she had used to support her three kids a single mom. She would lose it. Any opportunity to get a new car if this one died would be gone. Rent or mortgage payments would go unmet. With an uncertain job market, steady employment was a gift. I was asking her to choose life when it would cost her so much?

Slowly I began. "You don't know me. I wish you did. If you knew me, you would know that you could trust me. Like if I was your aunt or mother...you could believe me! I know so many people that would love to help you. We can help financially and in so many other ways. Could you just hold off on your decision? I see your little guy doesn't have a car seat. Let's start by me going to get you a brand new one. I can go today...and then get it to you tomorrow. It just doesn't seem like you really want to go through with an abortion. Let us help you! Please just trust me." Slowly I saw her head give a little nod. "Okay. I won't go into the clinic today."

"Father! She's not going to do it! Oh, I'm so happy. Nothing thrills me more than this amazing moment we now share in seeing a life rescued. I know that there will be much work to do. I'm going to need all Your strength and guidance and perfect ideas. This little family is going to need many, many people to come alongside them. I could never do it alone. But for now, for these next few hours, for today, her little baby is safe. Protect her dear baby. She obviously didn't really want to have the abortion. She is in a desperate corner, Father. Only You know the best way to get her out. I am utterly dependant on Your leading and help. Her future and my connection to it is in the shadows right now. I may not see clearly for some time. But I know, oh how I know, that You are able to do more than I can imagine."

Slowly the young woman left our parking lot. We could never have envisioned the journey ahead!

I WILL ALWAYS REMEMBER THIS DAY: This amazing young woman is now my friend. Our ministry and many others have walked beside her as she began to make good choices in her life. She attended a Bible Study each week and met other single moms that were struggling too. She quit her job as an exotic dancer. She began attending church and involved all her kids in the programs there. She was helped financially so she could purchase an apartment building with three units. She lives in one, and with the rent from the others as income, she now lives her life-long dream of being a stay-at-home mom. She attends college part time. Recently she was baptized and would love to start a Bible study with the dancers that work where she used to. On the day that my friend chose life, God knew that she would soon choose Real Life too. And He knew something else. He knew that the growing child in her womb was precious in His sight…and that his momma would name him…Angel.

The Saddest Tale Of All

I'm often asked, "What is the saddest story of all your years on the sidewalk?" I doubt very much if I do this work another twenty years that a more disturbing saga will present itself. It is unsettling in its display of spiritual confusion. It is horrific in its audacity to demand life go as planned… whatever the cost. And it's staggering to realize that it is not an isolated case. The story took place during the weeks we were restoring our Ministry House that God had provided (see page 85 for this amazing story!). That meant that although I wasn't on the sidewalk counseling, I was on site as the other counselors made valiant efforts on the clients' behalf.

She was young — 16 years old. She was home schooled and a Christian. And a liar. She had told her mom that she was driving to our city, an hour from her home, to attend a Christian concert. But that day she was really standing before a judge to get a judicial waiver for her abortion. In this state, if you are under 18 years old, you simply have to tell a judge why an abortion is just plain necessary for your mental health. All you need is a signed consent form and your parents never will be told about the abortion. The young woman told the counselors "I don't want my mom to know because she is a Christian and will make me keep this baby".

So a week after the day she stood before a judge, she was back at the clinic. It turned out that she was so far along – over 5 months – that she would have to be given a 2-day abortion. On this particular Thursday morning she would need to have laminaria inserted. Then she would go into labor all that following night. By Friday morning she would finally be "rid of her problem". During her three visits to the clinic, so many counselors tried to convince her of the dangers to her and of course her baby. So many prayer warriors prayed. But as with our ancient sister Eve, having life our own way is too powerful a prospect for some to resist. I often think of that Garden of Eden experience.

God Himself was Eve's Constant Companion. The world was perfect. She lived in blissful relationship with her husband. But still the allure of crafting the world your way on your terms proved too powerful to relinquish.

And so it was with the young Christian teen. This young woman had plans. She had her future mapped out and nothing or no one would stand in her way. In just a few months she wanted to enter Bible College. She knew that they would not accept a pregnant single woman. So her baby had to go. Plain and simple. Her young boyfriend was already at the college and she wanted to join him there.

She returned on Friday morning in great agony. She had been in labor all night and was in a great deal of pain. One of the counselors came into the Omega House where I was working and asked if she could lay down on one of the beds. What a moment that was. She…the one who lied and deceived to be the first to use the ministry House?? She…who chose self…and denied her own dear child the opportunity of life? Yes, I decided…that very one should be allowed to come in so we could minister to her. The counselor hurried out to give this hurting girl the news.

At that point the young woman was making her way into the clinic. She had decided to finish out her labor in their building. For the next hours we continued to pray for her. We had a pretty good idea what she must be experiencing at the hands of the doctor. At three o'clock that afternoon she emerged from the abortion clinic. I was working in an upstairs room, and could see her approach the place where we normally stand. She came to speak with the counselor one last time. Still in denial of the deed she had done, she mentioned the 'good news'. In her words: "Well it's over…but the good news is that I have a picture of my daughter. They gave me another ultra sound today, so I have a picture to keep. And she was sucking her thumb. Oh, I've named her. Her name is Victoria."

I WILL ALWAYS REMEMBER THIS DAY: Haunted by the image of a perfectly normal looking young woman, discussing seemingly casually her now dead daughter Victoria, sucking her thumb in utero just before her body would be removed by the doctor. And to find out later she also shared her goal to become a Youth Pastor after her stint at the Bible College. She felt that her experiences throughout the last week would help her empathize more with Youth and their problems. The thought of little Victoria alone in that building, with the remnant of life keeping her small body still warm for a time, threatens to undo me even today. Precious, beautiful infant life.
God have mercy on us all.

Praying Grandmas

A phenomenal occurrence happened a few years ago in our city. Some Grandmothers decided to get very serious about praying for the unborn and their mothers. That may not sound like much...but wait until you hear what happened! It's an amazing story!

I was the speaker at a conference for women. As I came in front of the podium to speak, I had my first glance at the audience. Of the three to four hundred in attendance, two thirds appeared to be over seventy. Many were in their eighties and had arrived on the buses from their retirement homes. Immediately I realized what a great opportunity to enlist prayer support for the sidewalk counseling ministry. These Godly Grandmas perhaps had a little more time to pray than busy young mothers. They had walked the Kingdom journey for many years. They had seen hundreds of answers to prayer over their lifetimes. What a prayer team they could be! As I looked out over this wonderful group of women, I told them that to my knowledge, I didn't have much prayer support on Wednesday mornings at the abortion clinic. As I began to explain what life was like on the sidewalk of that awful place, I could see that they were moved. Then I told them that I would be so comforted to know that as they thought about me on that morning, they would pray. I could never imagine what was about to take place!

It was Wednesday again, and twelve women came to the clinic for abortions. They were all inside the building as the time approached for the doctor to arrive. As I waited on the side of the building for his car to appear, I heard car doors slam. I ran to the parking lot...and all the clients were getting in their cars! I just stared at them! Then I asked where they were going. One of the women answered "We all have to leave because for some reason the doctor can't get here today." Can't get here?! He is literally unable to come over here and begin the abortions?!

"Father! I have never heard of such a thing. In ten years of counseling, there has never been a time when a doctor didn't show up! As I watch every client leave, my mind is numb. What is different today, Lord? Why now after all these years am I witnessing a complete breakdown of "business as usual"? 0 my! It's dawning on me...the Grandmas are praying!! All those dear saints who I asked to pray for me last week are doing just that. I have heard stories about the power of prayer. And now You are allowing me to see with my own eyes with what swiftness The Almighty God hears and answers prayer. I'm going home to call the nursing homes to notify my new prayer team, what has just happened!"

The next Wednesday, nine women came for abortions. They were all inside the building as the time approached for the doctor to arrive. As I waited on the side of the building for his car to appear, I heard car doors slam. I ran to the parking lot...and all the clients were getting in their cars! I just stared at them! Then I asked where they were going. One of the women answered "We all have to leave because for some reason the doctor can't get here today." Can't get here?! He is literally unable to come over here and begin abortions?!

"Lord! What IS this?! Exactly like last week?! Can it be? I am in total shock. Last week I was so honored to be a part of Your Divine intervention. And now this week You have allowed me to see Your power once again! O Father, no babies will die here today. No women will be wounded for life. I am so utterly humbled. I'm going home now to let the Grandmas know!"

The next Wednesday, eight women came for abortions. They were all inside the building....O my!!

"Mighty God! It has happened again. A complete shut down! No doctor! No abortions!! You have been totally victorious at this horrible place once again! I am so overwhelmed that I am weak from what I have just seen.

Bless the dear Grandmas for their diligence in prayer. I will always tell their story. So many believers are living their lives today as though no children were scheduled to die in their city. But a few faithful have earnestly come before You."

One more time I witnessed this marvelous event. The day it happened was a stormy Wednesday morning that probably looked ordinary enough to most people. But it was anything but that! I had fought the wind and the rain all morning. My umbrella was often inside-out. I had spoken with all the clients as best as I could under the wet circumstances. The prospect of having a "turn-around" seemed as gloomy as the skies above me looked.

Then suddenly, once again, every client left the clinic abruptly. One by one they started their cars and silently drove away. I didn't ask where they were going this time. I didn't ask why. I knew. God had intervened. As Grandmas prayed fervently that lives would be spared, He rushed in. He blew passed the locked door of the clinic and brought hope inside. He whirled through the procedure room and declared that no children would die here this day. He commanded in the waiting room that it was time to leave. The gods of self and convenience were sent scurrying. The doctor was stopped at a distant location. The staff was left bewildered that it had happened again.

And down on the sidewalk I fell to my knees. With the rain pouring down, I knelt in a puddle of water and wept. I cried because I knew that the Grandmas cared as much as I did. I cried because I finally had hope that this dreadful place maybe wouldn't last forever. I cried because I serve the Living God, Ruler of all, the Mighty Jehovah, my dearest Father. All the way home that day I wept. I released years of frustration and hurt from a call that has been hard. I had seen the Lord, high and lifted up! Praise be to Him!

I WILL ALWAYS REMEMBER THIS DAY: Within weeks of that dramatic day, the clinic closed for good. It never reopened as an abortion clinic. But it DID open as a church! Yes! That place where so many children were sacrificed is now a church. In this place of death the Word of Life is proclaimed. In this place of tears, children's voices ring out in laughter. I had the privilege of standing in their worship center, the former procedure room, and sharing stories from my years of counseling. Suddenly I realized I was looking from the INSIDE out. I was seeing for the first time the view the staff and clients had of me all those years. I thanked God for being with me in some of the most important moments of my life on a humble sidewalk.

Heart To Heart

Perspectives From The Sidewalk

Introduction

In the many years I have been a sidewalk counselor, I have formed a certain perspective on abortion and our response to it. Because it has been legal in this country for over 45 years, it is almost difficult to think of our society without it. In many ways I wonder if we have become (but how is that possible?) "used to it". We are inundated with messages that declare that choice is good, even best!

I'm not sure if we who are profoundly pro-life are in the minority or not. But I think we must fight the temptation to act that way. When we succumb to the notion that our up-hill battle is too difficult, we are defeated in our call to right-thinking. When we entertain the thought, even for a second, that maybe abortion isn't always harmful, we betray God's heart. When we feel discouraged because our efforts seem futile, we relinquish hope.

Two deadly concepts that rule our age are relativism and tolerance. We see their tentacles reach into all areas of modern thinking. Right is right as we define it, and you'd better not challenge personal decision on anything! It has been shocking to watch people embrace such warped ideas. Abortion is a case in point. Our society has insured its availability and fostered its acceptance. Anyone disagreeing with the widespread practice of abortion for any reason, is deemed intolerant. In American society today, tolerance is indeed a favored god.

Right-thinking, staying true to God's heart, and grasping on to hope are all possible as we embrace Biblical truth. Our saving faith is born there, and our strength to live out that faith is forged in the promises and assurances that those sacred pages hold. Whether we are in the majority or minority opinion on the issue of abortion is of little consequence. Our responsibility to God's truth is clear. Millions of lives are depending on us to work tirelessly, and in so doing to show the world that we are a people of hope.

Did I Really See That?!

There are times when I'm standing in front of the abortion clinics that I actually wonder did I really see that? I guess 'stunned' is how I usually feel. Was that really a mother dragging her young daughter in apparently against her will? Is that emotional young man so distraught that he's crying over there? Is that young girl all alone on this horrific day of her life? That mother is acting so tenderly to her child in the car seat…how can she destroy his sibling in the clinic? How can that grandmother playing so lovingly with her toddler grandchild as she waits in the car stand idly by and let her daughter abort her next grandchild? Why is that woman letting her boyfriend virtually drag her in the door?

But, for me, there are five groups of women that disturb me like none other. I see them on nearly every shift. They often leave me almost speechless. Simply put they are the wealthy, the young mothers, the casual, the very-far-along in pregnancy, and the Christians.

One group of women that confuses my sensibilities is the wealthy. Does that surprise you, too? Simply put…they can afford to raise a child! The abortion clinic that I counsel outside of has mostly middle and upper middle class people that use it services. I've seen BMWs, Jaguars, Cadillacs, and a host of other expensive vehicles. These women, of course would need little of the help our ministry has to offer. They want for nothing. And apparently the one thing that threatens to undo their lives-as-they-want-it lifestyle, is the little baby they're carrying. We all know women who sacrifice daily to care for their children. I am always shocked at a woman's choice to abort when she can so easily afford to support her child very comfortably.

Then there is the woman that has already borne children. Often they will drive up with a child in his car seat in the back. Some time we see a soccer sticker on the back of their mini van. They see no contradiction in the fact that their other children are allowed to live…and their sibling will be aborted that morning. I always think of the other kids in school, having a normal day, while this horrendous act takes place. How in the world can their mom keep the secret when they walk in the door from school? Most likely these "already moms" have seen ultra sound pictures with their other pregnancies. She knows her unborn child just needs time to develop. Does this baby just seem too much for her? Or as one father put it "I already have my boy and girl…I don't need another one".

I'm often asked "What are the women's attitudes as they approach the clinic doors?" I have certainly seen sad. I often see quiet and reflective. I have heard from angry women as well. But then there is the next group that totally unnerves... the very casual. They act as if this was a dentist appointment. Or that it's a simple matter that will have absolutely no impact on their lives. These are the women that would probably yell rude remarks my way, or laugh and joke on the way into the building. They are most often accompanied by an equally irreverent support person who joins in all the laughter. It always makes me wonder if they have done any research at all of the effects of abortion on their lives. Have they truly given a moment's serious thought to this life-altering decision? This horribly somber day stands in stark contrast to the "it's-no-big-deal" person walking in front of me.

Don't you love the beauty of seeing a woman finally show in her pregnancy? There is so much promise in a woman five, six, or seven months along. But what if you were to see her at that late date walk into an abortion clinic to pay someone to take that life out of her? We see it all the time. Some women come to the clinic so far along that you can hardly believe what you are seeing right in front of you. Haven't they felt life? Don't they realize that in a few short weeks their baby would have an excellent chance at survival? By that time in the pregnancy many couples would be painting the nursery, joyfully getting ready for the new arrival. But sadly, until the ninth month of pregnancy, a woman can legally abort her baby. It doesn't take much imagination to picture what will transpire on the surgical table and the fierce impact it will have on this woman's soul.

By far the most disturbing "category" I meet at the sidewalk is what I call "announcing Christians". These are women who boldly wear a "Christian" shirt or proudly display a bumper sticker that declares the fact that they are a believer. We live in an area that hosts several Christian colleges. All but one has had students come to use the clinic's services. Women from nearly every denomination of churches in this city come to the clinics for their abortions. Often the clients will tell us that they're Christians, and then tell us where they attend church. But as they so often say "You just don't understand. This is something I HAVE to do." I have seen Bibles on the seat next to them…or crosses displayed...or WWJD apparel worn with no shame. I have heard "I would rather abort this baby than face my board of elders." Or "My dad's a Baptist preacher and I don't want him to know that I am pregnant." One woman told me that her boyfriend was a Youth Pastor from a large church and they didn't want the church to find out that she was pregnant. Recently an Amish girl and her mother, in full Amish dress, came to the clinic. They had hired a driver to take them there. He was unaware what this appointment was all about and had only been told that they needed to see a 'specialist'. Professing Christians throwing over everything they were ever taught or believed, to be able to continue a lifestyle that is more important to them than walking in the protective Love of God.

And so yes, sadly, I did really see that. A ruffle-free life easily paid for at the expense of a precious baby. A family kept small, just as the couple pictured it, with the newest sibling deemed disposable. A life-changing decision given so little thought that on the day of the child's demise, joking and a casual spirit are the displayed. A woman so far along that even from a distance her baby can be seen although the mother herself can't "see" the truth. And conviction traded for convenience as beliefs held dear are cast away with the same dispatch as the little one inside. I ache in my heart because the Giver of Life really saw it all too.

House Of Hope

It's not surprising of God to do surprising things, but sometimes it seems like they mostly happen to other people! You hear of amazing things going on in many believers' lives. But when it happens to you personally…it feels like "shocking joy". Not long ago our ministry enjoyed just such a blessing. Let's together rejoice in God's great provision!

One of the clinics we stand next to as we counsel women is in a beautiful Historic District of our city. Stately old homes line many of the streets. Just a few feet from this abortion clinic stands a one hundred and fifty year old mansion. It actually belonged to one of our city's mayors at one time. For many years the owners gave us permission to stand right on their property. But the time had come that they needed to sell it. They checked with other pro-life groups in the area…but no one wanted to purchase it.

Although our ministry had about thirty volunteers, our budget was very small. We used what little money people donated to us to purchase the literature we hand-out at the sidewalk. We were also able to help when a client who chose life for her baby was in a financial crisis and needed a little assistance. But to come up with the over $200,000 needed to buy a mansion was a little out of our league! I remember distinctly thinking "I am so glad we are able to use this property for free because I can't think of one possible way we would ever need or use a mansion!"

But God had other plans. In short order He impressed upon our board that we should go forward with purchasing this House. So with a few thousand dollars to our name, and the prayers of many people behind us, we went forward. Before the ink was dry on the agreement the Holy Spirit began pouring out ideas! We could use this strategic location…a few feet from an abortion clinic which kept the lights on in the building 24 hours a day…to host Youth Group meetings to educate our Christian youth on the horrendous consequences of abortion. They could actually look into the two surgical rooms. We could reach more young people if we hosted Purity weekends for young women. They could come to this beautiful home and in a quiet setting learn about the standards God has set down to protect their young lives.

We could reach-out to the post-abortive community as well. Maybe they could come for a weekend and we could have counselors explain God's mercy, forgiveness, and love for them. They could begin to realize that hope and healing was possible. The very women that we, as sidewalk counselors, had urged not to go through with their abortions could now be ministered to at this special place. The thought of having them lovingly surrounded by beauty and peace sounded just right!

And what a place of prayer this could be. The parlor room overlooks the abortion clinic. But it also has a perfect view of the sidewalk counselors as they attempt to reach the clients going into the building. Those that care so much about the preciousness of life would be right in the center of the struggle with us.

So there WAS a use for this beautiful home. But how would it ever get paid for? Until my dying day…this "shocking joy" I will never forget! God just took the whole worry of the project right out of our hands. We never had to really work at raising funds. We never had to worry about how long it might take. We didn't have to come up with a short list of millionaires. Wonderfully He continued to show us that this responsibility would be ALL His, ALL the way! With that settled in my feeble mind He began showing His miraculous power!

If you could have lived in my shoes for the next few months you would never doubt our Sovereign God again. The money literally poured in. Poured! We received thousands of dollars from people who had never given to the ministry before. One day a check for $85,000 arrived. To this day I have never even met the donor! Within ten weeks, our debt of over $200,000 was paid in full.

But there's more. So much needed to be done inside the House. It had been in a state of disrepair for some time. Volunteer help began to show up. Youth groups and retirees; young moms and grandmas; craftsmen and the not-so handy; all lent a hand! We painted and papered and fixed up and cleaned up. We replaced and repaired and re-arranged and restored. Along with the gift of hours of free labor came the gifts to furnish the House. Curtains, bedding, kitchen supplies, and furniture, joined the new lighting, plumbing, and carpet…all arriving in a steady stream day after day! God spared no expense. He took a Mayor's Mansion and restored it to be fit to serve The King.

At one time this Home was owned by another pro-life group. They had named it the Omega House. To me, that is still a fitting name. The word in the Greek alphabet is last…the end. I want this place, this gift of God to be truly the END of some things. As we educate our visitors about the clinic next door, I want it to be the end of pretending that abortion is not the tragedy I know it is. I want it to be the end of an often silent church that does not teach its young people that God holds them to a different standard than this culture projects…that God's way is the only safe route for their journey through this difficult life. I want the Omega House to help people escape a often complacent world view. And of course for the dear post-abortive women, so deceived or distracted by life that they chose to abort someone they can never replace, I want to facilitate true healing that will end their self-condemnation, guilt and shame.

The END. Because He is the OMEGA. Our Reigning King, who tells us He is the Alpha of all things… tells us He is the Omega too. The final Word. His redemption covers all our sins. His position at the Right Hand of the Father seals it all. The despair and heartache of a fallen world answers to Him. He has dominion and authority. When it is all over and every knee shall bow, our Hope for eternal life rest squarely in our Omega. Trust Him, dear Friend. What ever you need Him for today, He is eager to bring you "shocking joy" too!

A Stranger Passed Our Way

A stranger passed our way one day as we stood in front of the abortion clinic to counsel the women going inside. And we told him an awful lot. I wish we had never told him anything, really. His eyes still haunt me as I remember the horrified look on his face as we delivered our facts. He literally, physically staggered backwards. His mind could not accept what we so glibly offered.

The stranger turned out to be Jacob, hopefully to be Pastor Jacob someday he says! He was one of the "Lost Boys" of Sudan, Africa. A beautiful young man with jet-black skin, very tall and thin. He would stand out in any crowd. His hair was cropped close to his head. His smile was brilliant and warm. As he reached out to shake our hands, his strong grip enfolded us, his toughened skin a witness to many years of hard living. Several of these dear young people grace our city with their presence. They work in our stores, ride their bikes around town, and attend the local Community College. That's where we met Jacob. The abortion clinic shares the same four-corners as the college in the downtown area.

First our greetings were general. "We hope your having a good day ... how are your classes going? ... what are you taking?" And then came the question that seemed harmless enough. "My name is Jacob, and what are you ladies doing here?" Our answer was straight-forward, "This is our city's abortion clinic. Right here in this former church. We come here to help women." And then came a long piercing look of disbelief ... "What are you saying? They are killing children here?"

In a no-nonsense way we explained what goes on in the clinic. Many women come. They don't want to be pregnant anymore. Often the babies are quite large already because the women are almost 6 months along. And there we stood, three sidewalk counselors going through the litany of facts that we have shared dozens of times. Direct. Unflinching. A barrage of words that is so common to us all. Women come. Babies die. A doctor kills them. It is legal in America to kill babies up to the ninth month. Just words.

But not to Jacob. Not to sensitive, innocent Jacob. Presumably he had seen untold tragedies in his war-torn country. Perhaps he had seen his own parents killed before his very eyes. Most assuredly he had been on his own with the other orphan boys for many years. He had experienced the cruelty of man. He had tasted injustice. He had witnessed unimaginable sorrow. But this? This act of violence was too horrific to process in his pure mind.

"What are you saying that they are killing babies . . . here?!" "Are they killing the babies now?!" "Are they killing the babies in the church right now?!" "Who is that woman? She is the nurse? She is the nurse that helps in killing the babies?"

Over and over. In total disbelief.

"But don't the people know? Don't they know about God? Don't they know that this sin will be judged?"

Slowly, with those beautiful hands he demonstrated the opening of a book.

With great passion he implored us to understand ... "It is all written down! Someday God will show you the book of your life and all of it will be written down. And this too ... God knows this!"

O, Jacob. I... am ... so... sorry. I stood there with tears coming up from a deep place in my soul. In the presence of such innocence I could hardly bear to look into his face.

"But you must tell me ... why has America said you may kill the babies? Why has your country let the babies die?!"

And we just stood there . . . without words now. Three counselors totally wordless. Because we didn't know how to answer such a charge. Indeed . . . why?! How did it happen those many years ago? Who could have known what it would come to?

Unflinchingly he searched our faces for answers. But there were none. We stood in silence. His pain tore at my heart. Where had I seen that look before? Whose eyes could look so deep in to the hidden places? The busy downtown corner vanished in my sight and hearing. I stood there barely breathing. I wept in shame as I realized that I hadn't mourned enough. I hadn't sacrificially grieved God's indescribable loss. I stood there guilty. Guilty of working very hard to go on with my life as usual, even though I knew. Even though I knew that babies were dying in a church building by the whim of their mothers and the greed of a doctor.

But Jacob could not go on as though he didn't know. He fumbled for words of parting, but none came. He didn't know how to end a conversation that had told him more that he could bear. He silently began to back away from us. Shocked and dismayed. A "Lost Boy" discovered something in his new-found land that unnerved him more than the ravaged land he had left. A stranger passed our way one day... with a hauntingly familiar gaze.

God have mercy on us all.

It Takes All Kinds

I love the saying that it takes all kinds to make the world go around. We observe that truth all the time in our daily lives. So many different people add to the texture of our world. In great and small ways, all are needed to make things run smoothly. In recent years I have seen that in the pro-life movement as well. I had no idea how diverse the opportunity for service was. We tend to see only our own small part in things. I am in the circle of many wonderful women that are sidewalk counselors. But the list of contributions people make to rescue women and their babies is virtually endless!

Some people give forty hours a week to office and administration work, at a very low salary. In that faithful number are secretaries, receptionists, accountants and friendly voices that answer hundreds of phone calls. To help the office staff, scores of volunteers come to stuff envelopes and cheerfully assist where they can. Then there are the fund-raisers . . . what a job! No pro-life organization could do without them or the event coordinators that labor to arrange for special projects that "re-fill" the coffers! They are selfless in the hours they donate to come-up with creative ideas and then manage to pull them off too!

Add to that list those that work in educating the public and keeping them informed. Often they are visionaries who design and distribute well-written literature that informs but also captures the heart. Dynamic young people see the importance of reaching teens and staying on the cultural edge to appeal to youth before it is too late. There are also public relations people and media experts. They are careful to make sure that others understand our goals and objectives. Some men and women work through the legislature and push for laws that protect the unborn and their mothers. Capable people seek election in government, willing to risk all to take a stand for life even in politics.

Local congregations are filled with men and women that are eager to lend a helping hand. Church coordinators serve as liaisons to keep congregations well informed and engaged. Occasionally pastors and priests are willing to preach a sermon on life issues. Some members feel called to spend hours in prayer for all the heartache surrounding the abortion decision. Caring people give sacrificially to support women in unplanned pregnancies. Often they are willing to shower a young mother with all that she might need in her new life of added responsibility.

Dedicated men and women work in crisis pregnancy centers as well. With loving hearts they spend hours talking to abortion-minded women. Medical personnel often team up with these centers to give input and expert advice without financial benefit. Whatever concerns a frightened woman, they try to give advice and alleviate some of her stress. They gently tell the truth but are willing to still care for the client even if she chooses abortion. Brave post-abortive women share their devastating stories to minister to hurting women who have made the wrong choice. Help-line counselors and social workers in adoption agencies stand ready to listen. They carefully walk a young woman through the difficult process of releasing her little one for adoption.

I am so impressed with these people! And I am blessed to know many of them. With no thought of financial gain or personal comfort they "fight the good fight". How pleased the Lord must be with their generous hearts. They are relentless in their drive to keep the issues of life before a fickle society. God's Word tells us to count the cost of following His way... and they have. And after counting that cost, they make a dramatic statement with their own lives. The most vulnerable among us must be protected. All life is precious. It certainly takes all kinds to make the pro-life world go around...which kind are you?

I Wish You Had Been There

I observed an amazing scene at the abortion clinic the other day...I wish you had been there! It was a bright summer morning filled with warmth and sunshine. Every new day at the clinic brings the hope of a young woman's rescue from disaster and the longing of a baby's life saved from death. This seemed like any other day, but God gently pulled back the veil of the ordinary to show us the glory of walking with Him.

A sidewalk counselor knelt down on the street with her head against the clinic wall. She begged God to fight for them on this day of impending disaster for the clients scheduled. She asked that He send His mighty angels to place a hedge of protection around each woman as she struggled to make her decision today. She prayed for guidance and wisdom, for love and compassion. She admitted her great weakness and asked for Divine strength.

Across the street a faithful prayer warrior began his steady walk of prayer. Back and forth he calmly prevailed upon God to help us on this day. As always, his presence calmed the counselor's spirit... she was not alone. Before long, a young man took his place on the sidewalk. He had been there before and knew just what to do. He found a tree for shade, bowed his head, and went before God. "O, Lord... where two or three are gathered in Your Name... We are here now... listen to our cries!"

Soon he was joined by a wonderful group of young people. In their busy world, they managed to carve out time to pray. Amazingly they were willing to come before God on behalf of the young people their own age, who had chosen such a different lifestyle. Without judgment or condemnation, they simply began to pray. And now this fine group was joined by a family that also saw the need for prayer by this place of despair and death. They came, they knelt, and they began to fervently pray. Now our two or three was a mighty army!

But there was more. From around the corner came two grandmothers. They were taking a turn in the Upper Room prayer center to also go before God in earnest. They greeted the sidewalk counselors with a heartfelt promise to passionately pray for each woman and baby in danger at the clinic today. Their presence was a bless-ed assurance that God's people had heard His call to make a difference in this troubled world. With so much "prayer power" what was going to happen?

Oh... I wish you had been there to see what happened next! Suddenly we were all aware that a young couple was struggling to make the decision to go inside the clinic doors. They stood at the side of the building deep in conversation. They seemed unable to complete the journey into the clinic. All those that had come to pray were immediately united in a common goal...all hearts prevailed upon our Great God to rescue and save!

A half hour stretched into an hour. They still were in tortured indecision. Several times the counselors approached them. Often they backed off to give them "space". An hour stretched into two. Still they talked. Still we prayed. At one time my eyes swept over this amazing scene. Precious saints of God, from twelve years old to eighty, all pouring themselves into intercession on behalf of total strangers. From the prayer room to the sidewalk on both sides of the street, the faithful yearned to see this young couple turn and leave.

And then it happened. They simply left! After a morning of indecision their hearts had been moved to leave the clinic, never having gone inside! I wish you had been there to see the tears in the eyes of the prayer warriors when they heard the news. I wish you had been there to see them look up with hearts of gratitude and faces of joy and exclaim "Thank You, Jesus!" I wish you had been there to see our Mighty God burst in on a scene on impending disaster and declare "I have heard your cries... I am Jehovah, the God Who saves!" I wish you had been there.

I've Heard It All

Through the years on the sidewalk I think I have heard it all. I'm always interested in the reasons men and women give for making the decision to abort their child.

Some tug at the heart:

I am alone
I am scared
I am ashamed

Some reveal the panic a woman feels:

My parents would kill me
I've had an affair and don't want people to find out
I don't have any insurance

Some blame others:

My mom insisted that I come
My pastor said I should do this
My girlfriends convinced me that it was no big deal

Some point-out the lies of a godless culture:

It's my right to choose life or death
It's so small that it's not even a baby yet
It's better to abort the baby than give it up for adoption

Some display an unbelievably selfish attitude:

I don't want to lose my figure
I just started a new job, and don't want to give it up
I'm too young to be tied down

Some put fear in my soul:

> I prayed about it and know it's God's will
> This way God can just take care of it in Heaven
> I know God will forgive me anyway

As I see women enter the clinic doors, it's important that I listen to their stories. They must know that I am trying to hear their hearts. Through the years I have been convinced that there is great turmoil in the souls of most women who come to this decision. But sadly, some seem almost indifferent to what is about to take place. Others seem to want to accept our culture's assertion that personal rights must be paramount. "My rights first" seems so plausible to them. And, tragically, there are also a large number of women who seem to be in deep denial until the procedure is over.

I've heard it all on Wednesday mornings. Each week a parade of women pass in front of me. Their troubled lives are caught-up in culture, calamity, and chaos. And lost in that turmoil is someone who cannot be reasoned away. When it is all over, their little ones' absence will tear at a place that no justification can heal.

Tipping The Scales

I have this interesting image in my head of how the prayer of the saints tips the scale, spiritually speaking. I picture one of those old-fashioned scales with the weights on one side, and the item to be weighed balancing it on the other. A single committed believer can outweigh all the schemes of the evil one. I've seen it happen dramatically only twice in our ministry. The first time was when a group of grandmas were challenged to pray for the sidewalk ministry, just dear sweet grandmas. But as they began to petition God on our behalf, there was such an outpouring of His visible power that we were all stunned. Within months of their faith-filled prayers ascending to the throne of God, the abortion clinic closed its doors.

Just a few months ago, I spoke at a church during their Sunday School hour. It was an important opportunity to explain the abortion industry and the work we do in front of the clinic. We ended our time together with a question and answer period. With just a few minutes to go before my time was up, a woman asked an innocent enough question. "What can we do for YOU, as sidewalk counselors?" I had never been asked that before. I thought about it for a few seconds. It was asked so sincerely with obvious intent to follow through. So I answered simply, "We need to be adopted."

Adopted? Yes, adopted. We needed to find a home in peoples' hearts. We needed to be remembered on those difficult days in front of the clinic. We needed assurance that God's people would bring our names and ministry into His Matchless Presence.

And that was when the scale was tipped. People took my honest response to heart. Since that day, when the members of that church pledged to intercede for us, our world at the clinic has been turned upside down. It was as though God had said, "Is there any man or woman willing to invest part of their lives into these counselors' work? Do I see the hand of just one person that will pledge to pray? Because if you do, it will make all the difference." Suddenly it didn't matter if satan and his ruthless gang wanted to thwart our attempts at sharing God's love. It was of no consequence if the clinic was his kingdom and we were intruders. A group of common homemakers was about to see the strength of God released.

That small group of intercessors opened the floodgates of blessing for us. Soon encouragement came from all over the city. A woman volunteered to recruit dozens of prayer warriors to pray for our ministry, and they meet regularly in the Upper Room prayer center. Through a specific request, hundreds of people have pledged to pray for the closing of the clinic and the salvation of the doctor that does the abortions. Large groups of people came faithfully each week to pray on the street across from the clinic as well. New sidewalk counselors signed on to help with great enthusiasm. Finances came in for the purchase of literature.

And lives were saved! So many babies have been saved that we have had to write them all down just to keep track of their stories! Women have changed their minds about getting an abortion before they even enter the building. And we have seen their tears of relief and joy as they realize how close they came to disaster.

Can just one more praying person make that big a difference? Can a tiny group of believers effect that much change? You will never convince me otherwise. I am living through a time of tipped scales . . . and the blessings are tumbling out all around me.

A Day Of Hope

Against a very dark background, the experience of hope is especially meaningful. It's a testimony to the God-image within us I think. We see our world and its difficult realities. We live through trying situations and taste despair. We sense no clear direction for our future. We feel overwhelmed and close to being submerged in our circumstances. We come close to giving up and giving in. But then an astounding emotion pushes up through our souls . . . HOPE!

On one level or another, we've all felt it. A job interview goes better than expected . . . and we have hope for our future. A medical test comes back negative . . . and our spirits are lifted. There is reconciliation with a loved one . . . and all is right with the world! A baby smiles for the first time . . . and bright promise fills us with joy. A rainy day clears up; a bad cold goes away; a child's tears are turned to laughter . . . HOPE!

We in the pro-life community, at our very core, are hopeful people. For most of us it's our Source that keeps us looking around the bend for that surprising oy. We care so deeply for the child in the womb. We want to be the solution to all the problems that bring a young woman to an abortion clinic. We passionately try to educate those in our community about the truth of abortion. But there are times we wonder if we will lose our way. Will things ever be different?

I think you should know about something that I experienced recently. It was a special day . . . a day of hope. Initially this seemed like just a regular Wednesday. It dawned in an ordinary way. But by nightfall everything was different! The building that houses the largest abortion clinic for miles around has been for sale for years. No one has wanted to purchase it. It has been in disrepair, and of course has quite a reputation. It's the clinic where we sidewalk counsel. Week after week business has been going on as usual. Several times there were rumors of a sale. . .but it never happened. Then one day. . .there it was. . .a SOLD sign on the building!! Can you imagine our joy?! Immediately the story came out that a few brave Christian businessmen were helping to purchase it for a pro-life organization. After years and years of praying, things could finally change.

I immediately thought of one of my favorite stories in the Old Testament. Maybe you, too, have compared our struggle against the culture of abortion to the account of David and Goliath. I think it is an apt one. What must those other well-trained soldiers have felt as David approached the huge, pagan enemy? Certainly there had to be anxiety and fear for his life. Some must have doubted a good outcome. But I wonder if deep inside there was a tiny place of hope. After all the bad, could good prevail? At a time when they felt totally helpless, was victory in sight? Would the little warrior with great faith be enough to quell the shouts of a fearsome foe?

God's resounding answer to His people was "Yes, there is hope . . . in Me!" And His answer is the same to us. We, too, struggle against strong opposition. We shed tears for a world gone desperately wrong. We long for women to understand the truth before it is too late. We grieve for babies lost. We desire for the staff of abortion clinics to have a true change of heart. We educate and legislate. And we pray . . . oh how we pray!

And then one ordinary day, it happens. Right before the eyes of His faithful people, God does a mighty work! Suddenly all the years of hurt and frustration vanish as hope is birthed in our hearts. "SOLD". . . one word so full of meaning. "Goliath is down!" "The enemy is on the run!" "God is victorious!"

As you continue to work in earnest to rescue women and their unborn babies . . . may God comfort you with the words, "Your day of HOPE is coming!"

The Garden Of Hope

After many years on the sidewalk I began to sense a slight shift in my focus. When I began to get involved with the ministry, I certainly cared deeply for the little babies that were discarded through abortion. That's what brought me to the sidewalk in the first place. But through personal interaction with so many of their mothers, I began to ache for what they went through as a result of their abortion.

Some Wednesday mornings I was able to spend a great deal of time reaching out to these women. If they were willing to talk I did my best to caution them about the dangers of what they were about to do. Most clients had to wait three hours before they had their abortion. During that time some would share what was in their hearts and how afraid they felt. I began to see clearly what that expression "between a rock and a hard place" really meant. I saw mothers and boyfriends literally pull these women into the clinic. I saw tears and heard details of a life gone very wrong.

Nothing clutched my heart more than seeing these same women leave a few hours later. By now their faces were etched in my memory. I worried, even as they were on the abortionist's table, that he would do them serious physical harm. As they left the clinic to return to their car, many of them were in tears. Often it was painful for them to even make that walk to their vehicle. Slowly, almost in a daze, they opened the car door. Gingerly they sat down.

As I watched them drive away from the clinic my heart broke. Often they didn't even speak to the one who brought them. Usually they laid their head back or slumped against the window. What had just transpired in their souls was plainly displayed through their body language. They left the clinic forever changed. Life would never be the same.

I found myself praying a benediction on them, "The Lord bless you and keep you". Keep you from sinking into utter despair. Keep you from participating in a frantic and destructive lifestyle in an attempt to dull the memory of today. Keep you from further torture at the hand of satan who is gleeful about today and full of ideas to terrorize tomorrow.

I felt desperate to reach these dear women. I remember thinking, "How can I find them all back?! Someone needs to hold them and assure them of their worth. Who will tell them that there is forgiveness? How will they find hope?" Somehow they had to hear words of comfort for their troubled souls. God impressed upon me to do something quite unusual. With the help of hundreds of people in the pro-life community we built the Garden of Hope.

The primary purpose of this unique garden is to reach out to women that have had abortions. It is a beautiful place! Carefully landscaped to provide a place of quiet refuge, every detail says "You are treasured". In the center of the garden is a breath-taking piece of artwork. A life-size sculpture depicts Jesus, sitting next to a young woman, holding her hand. He cradles her baby tenderly in His arm. There is an obvious look of compassion and understanding on His face. Every visitor can sense the welcoming grace of Jesus in this piece.

I believe that the sidewalk ministry has come full circle. Many years ago we were desperate to save babies. And we still are. But we also long to touch their mothers. Certainly before they enter the clinic doors we try to offer help. But now, as they leave that building where the nightmares begin, we gently hand them literature on post-abortion. Surprisingly they will often stop to talk. They know that we know. They look at us to see what will be written on our faces now. And there is only one thing, compassion. The love of Christ compels us to minister to "the still bleeding ones" just minutes after their abortion. With tender sadness we give them a picture of the Garden of Hope and explain that it was built with love, just for them. Disbelieving that someone still finds them of value, they quietly thank us and walk towards an uncertain future.

The Garden of Hope

www.gardenofhope.com

A Final Thought

Often people want to know what they should do after they have been touched by these face to face encounters. My answer is always the same. We must be willing to grieve about the things that grieve the Heart of God. We must mourn for this unspeakable sorrow in our world. Every child lost to abortion was a unique creation of our Great God. Every man and woman involved in the abortion experience are at some level wounded for life. They must be loved and restored.

Perhaps you have been encouraged to ask God what He wants you to do in this area. We have over 30 men and women that help us in our ministry in front of abortion clinics. Rarely is it a comfortable or easy place to minister.

God might have something entirely different in mind for you. Our society is in dire need of "salt and light" in the area of abortion. God can use your unique personality and gifts to be a help and comfort to struggling men and women.

May I say that if you are a person that has been through the abortion experience, I want you to know that you are dearly loved by God. My heart felt prayer is that nothing in this book wounds you further. The wonderful truth of God is that in repentance you may embrace His sure mercy and forgiveness. His desire is that you come to complete healing. His offer to you today is . . . hope . . . please accept it from His gracious hand.

Going Before God

Prayer Beyond The Sidewalk

Introduction

One of the greatest blessings our ministry enjoys, are the hundreds of people that pray for us and our concerns. There literally is the need for prayer daily, in regards to the impact abortion has in our society.

On the following pages I have included some of the prayer updates that have been sent-out to our faithful friends. Sometimes we have great needs as a ministry and sometimes we just want to praise God together.

Following the update section, I will also give some "prayer ideas" for you as you bring these issues before God within your church family, or in your own personal time.

garden
where mercy meets hope
of hope

December 18, 2015

Dear Praying Friends,

I have a Christmas Present for you! A pull-back of the earthly curtain to see our Sovereign God intricately weave the moments of this very morning into a perfect scene to exhibit His love and power! I am still shaking my head about it all hours later!

I am almost never "on the wall" on Friday morning. Remember the young woman we helped in the last few weeks with car repairs etc.? Today we planned to meet to help her out with phase two of her difficulties:). She lives pretty far away so was willing to meet halfway at the Omega House. When I arrived I was in the middle of some chaos! I was told the usual sidewalk counselor had just taken someone to a Crisis Pregnancy Center, and a couple of people up front had been talking to a woman who parked up the hill. In the space of a couple of minutes she walked into the clinic...and out again!

Suddenly they asked if I could jump into the dialogue with her. I saw her walk down our driveway and I asked if she trusted me enough to sit in the car with me. She did:) As soon as she was in the warm car she began to cry. She had desperately tried to get her $200 back form the abortion clinic ultrasound... but they refused to give it to her. She even said they implied she may as well stay for the abortion because she had that money tied up anyway! She said "I just can't go back in there. I have for sure changed my mind!"

Here's the beautiful part I told her..."You don't have to! Our ministry refunds the money to you because the clinic won't!" More tears...that was her only other child's "Christmas money" for gifts. More beauty...I said "Oh that's covered too!" A church just gave us a "gift card shower" and I have them along with me. Their sole purpose was to bless women just like her:)

And here's the sweet, sweet detail I loved! Earlier in the morning was Christmas baking time. I had a too-yummy-to-believe coffee cake with me in the car. The whole car smelled homey and delicious. So this dear soul left with gift cards, the promise of help for the next several months, the promise of all the baby furniture she needed, the promise that the $200 check will be in the mail this very day, and super comfort food (which she noticed with delight..."it's still warm!").

When I returned home after meeting the other young woman too...and sending them both off with grandmotherly hugs and assurances...I found a gift waiting for me! In it was a very cool bracelet that said "BELIEVE". As much as I wanted it...who needed it more?? Yup! So with the check is a bracelet, too, to encourage her and point her to The One that went out of His way to show her His lavish love and care!

Think of the complicated details that were put in perfect order by " GOD WITH US...IMMANUEL" for one impoverished woman and her tiny baby. Think of how the angels must have rejoiced to see God emphatically win in the struggle between good and evil. Think how He put just the right crowd together for this event. Think of the refuge from the cold He provided as she sorted everything out. Think how He sent her gifts to encourage her. O Come Let Us Adore HIM!

Mary

garden of hope
where mercy meets hope

March 5, 2016

Dear Praying Friends,

I waited a couple of days to share this because it almost falls in the category of "Did I see and hear this right?" On Wednesday morning a very expensive vehicle drove into the clinic lot. It appeared to be a grandma and her granddaughter. Parking was tight so they left the abortion clinic parking lot to find another place. But what was so strange is that they repeated that behavior three times! They couldn't seem to just park, and walk into the clinic.

One time they drove down the driveway at the Omega House. They backed up as to park...but never shut off the engine. As I approached the car I noticed that both women were crying... usually a very good sign of a conflicted heart. Now that I look back on it, I don't think either women actually spoke. They nodded their head, or silently shook it to say "no" to a question, but I never heard their voices. I asked several questions to try and determine what was the main cause of their grief. But after taking our information packet, they quietly left. Sadly, after all that, they re-parked in the clinic's lot and went in the building.

Whenever we see tears we are actually encouraged! Clients have told us that they try to stay numb until the abortion is over, Several people were praying out front as part of the 40 Days for Life campaign. So for quite some time I believe our prayers were focused on these distressed women. After about an hour more my shift was up and I had guests that came down the see the Omega House and hear about Garden of Hope Ministry. Probably after two hours from initially seeing this expensive car show up, the next sidewalk counselor on duty came into the prayer room and announced "They left!! The grandma said she is NOT having the abortion!!" I sort of, kind of, SCREAMED! (Felt bad for my guests) After so long in the abortion clinic, and after parking and re-parking three times...she changed her mind?? It had been so long! They had never said they had doubts about going through with it!

No fancy words from us, no laid out plans to aide and assist, for the best reason of all she left... GOD WORKED IN HER HEART AND SHE OBEYED! The words of Psalm 67 kept going through my head for the rest of Wednesday:"May the people praise You, O God; may all the people praise You." On Fulton Street, on the Wall, in the Omega House prayer room, throughout the city as people heard..."You did it Father! Only YOU! A broken-hearted grandma and her distressed granddaughter came to a place of death in tears, and went home with LIFE!"

To SEE if before our eyes is so humbling. Join me in praising HIM today!

Mary

garden of hope

where mercy meets hope

March 26, 2016

Dear Praying Friends,

On this day before Easter, rejoice with us in these precious snapshots of one week in the life of our ministry where God shown through so brightly! Gems of hope that encourage our hearts!

On Friday…a day so dark for our Savior…He brought HOPE by having a couple leave their clinic appointment and returning to their home with their baby safe from satan's evil plan for destruction.

On that same day, over twenty people came to Fulton Street in front of the clinic to worship God and pray earnestly to Him.

With some of our counselors sick, God provided for every shift to be filled by His dear faithful daughters who so willingly accept this hard ministry of sidewalk counseling. Precious in His sight are these women!

In just a five-day period, God enlisted the aid of Cradles of Grace, Hope Unexpected, Alpha Women's Center of G.R., and Lowell and Family Life Center to be at the ready for those who contacted us this week.

An almost humorous list of others in the community aided us too: the Orkin man, a harried mother of three that juggled her schedule to meet up with a client about to have her power services cut-off to give the money needed, a willing grandpa who met a client to bless her with gift cards, a tow truck operator who found a disabled car for us, a mechanic and his right-hand man who managed to pull off an extraordinary fix on that same car, and a very busy mom who spent hours texting and calling to smooth troubled hearts that thought abortion was their only answer.

And finally, two of our "former clients"...who still communicate with us…plan to be in God's House tomorrow on Easter! Pray that their souls are gripped to hear the Good News!

In many ways the events of this week seemed overwhelming…many huge needs and difficult circumstances. God met every need in truly bright and shining ways. We humbly thank our Risen Lord for continuing year after year to show us His steadfastness and remind us why we're very glad we use "HOPE" in our ministry name!

Have a Blessed Easter, faithful friends!

Mary

garden of hope
where mercy meets hope

August 10, 2017

Dear Praying Friends,

I learned recently that when the word "victory" is used in biblical settings, it more precisely means that the victory was only possible because of God's direct intervention. I'm sure we have all experienced that amazing truth!

A battle raged at the clinic yesterday between a stepmother and her daughter. The stepmom was 100% insistent that the young woman go into the clinic to abort her baby. The young couple had "accidentally" come into the Omega house parking lot:-) How we love that! For the next 45 minutes the stepmother yelled and swore and threatened from the clinic parking lot below. In between all of her outbursts she constantly texted the boyfriend and her daughter's phone and called them as well. It was utter turmoil. I invited the couple to speak with us further in the Omega House, but out of fear, she didn't want to leave her car. To complicate matters the young man worked for this girl's father. So by choosing life he could lose his job and cut off all relationship with the parents.

Slowly I was able to observe a strong man, a Hero, emerge right before my eyes. I watched as the boyfriend took on the responsibility of going to the wall and speaking with the stepmother. Then he answered all the incoming texts and phone calls. And finally he told the out-of- control woman that it was time for her to go. They had decided to have this baby!

Throughout the battle, it was so beautiful to see God bring in reinforcements! My prayer partner of over 15 years began to speak with the shouting woman. I know him well enough to know he was able to challenge her on some important things. And right in the middle of everything else a client - who actually had her baby later that afternoon! - came to receive the gift of a security deposit for her new place to live. As she left the Omega House parking lot she told this young woman face-to-face not to abort.

And our favorite reinforcement, the young couple went to Alpha Women's Center to get an ultrasound. There they saw a very active baby and found out that she was entering her fourth month of pregnancy.

Oh the victory is HIS! I know in the weeks ahead there will be many things this young couple needs. But I know that the God Who rescued is the God Who provides. And the God Who won the battle is the God Who will bring them safely through!

Grateful beyond words for all of you. :-)

Mary

garden of hope
where mercy meets hope

July 18, 2017

Dear Praying Friends,

Sometimes our time spent with the women outside the abortion clinic is very brief. In the scope of things, we only have a tiny glimpse into their lives. In a very concise way I would like to mention three families we have met in the last several days...and joyfully report on a fourth.

1. One young woman came, she was spoken to and then accepted the invitation to go to Alpha Women's Center. God provided an escort for her to guide her all the way there:-) we don't know the results at this time.

2. A mother brought her daughter to the clinic last week. She was okay with speaking with the sidewalk counselors, and shared that she had been raised in church and that she herself had been through an abortion. She was upset with this turn of events with her own daughter. Her daughter's life is very difficult and she needs help with babysitters and finances. Of course, and now too she will be dealing with the grief over her abortion.

3. This morning, Tuesday, a couple came to the clinic with what seemed like obvious financial need. As we told them the many ways Garden of Hope has been blessed by God's people, so that we can in turn help women in crisis, they were actually in shock:-) But they left the parking lot with their little12 week old baby safe and secure! We will now begin the process of sorting through their current situation of need.

4. Cassandra's baby comes home this week :-) She will resume her job again very soon.

Four women.... All different situations.... All different journeys. Aren't you glad that the God we love and serve promises the opposite of a "brief glimpse" into our lives? He is The Blessed Pervasive Presence that never leaves or forsakes!

Mary

garden of hope
where mercy meets hope

March 9, 2018

Dear Praying Friends,

I wanted you to see this picture I took on this week's snowy Wednesday morning.

A mother and daughter approached the wall after having been in the clinic for about 20 minutes. If you can see it, there are two sets of footprints. The one on the left is that of the very concerned mother. She must have been pacing back and forth the whole time we talked. The one on the other side is that of her daughter who had come to the clinic to abort her baby. She just stayed in one place, almost paralyzed with the enormity of her decision: Life or death. Parent or adoption.

Something else hit me about this picture. It shows the trash can of the clinic on the left. And right behind where they stood is the doctor's very expensive car. What it doesn't show is that straight up on that third side was a video camera observing our every move. In effect this mother and daughter were surrounded on all sides with dark symbols of the clinic. The precious babies are treated as trash. Money is the motivator for this horrific practice. And the video camera reminds us that we are being scrutinized as the "enemy" every second we stand for Life.

And then it hit me... God overcame it all! Right there, in view of the camera, the young woman chose life. Right there they allowed me to pray over them. And right there she made her decision to visit Bethany Christian Services that very day! That is The God we serve! He doesn't care how impossible it looks. He doesn't care if it seems like evil surrounds us. He wants this amazing truth to sink into into our daily lives: He is in control. Always. Forever.

Nehemiah 9:5-25 is a glorious passage of praise for all God had done. I read it...and then re-read it putting in events of this precious day. With JOY I re-affirmed through this prism of amazement that Jehovah is from everlasting to everlasting!

Mary

garden of hope
where mercy meets hope

May 7, 2018

Dear Praying Friends,

It began with a look around the backyard of the Omega House with flowers blooming, leaves beginning to come out, and one particular robin who would not give up singing his cheerful song! He literally perched on the fence at the side of the parking lot and sang his little heart out! Eventually, I could not help but join him... a song of praise amid all the darkness and sadness we see at the clinic doors. So as the morning went on - with joy - I thought of the many things we have to be thankful for in our ministry! Here are a few:

1. Faithful sidewalk counselors who just came through a brutal winter and never missed a shift. :)
2. The gift of willing hands to help us with some of our bigger projects. Most recently: grounds clean up around the Omega house, complete with flowers planted and multiple bags of yard waste removed. :)
3. The promise of more help to come throughout the summer to keep the Garden of Hope beautiful as well.
4. Several babies born healthy, beautiful, and deeply appreciated by their mothers!
5. "Final chapters" written with some of our young moms... good jobs found, roofs over their heads, well-running vehicles to assist them, food on the shelves, and so many sharing about their church attendance!
6. Recent interest by several pastors in our post-abortive Bible studies....and a great willingness to share this information with the women of their Church.
7. The precious gift of financial donations...always enough to help every woman that changes her mind.
8. New inquiries from women considering the possibility of being trained as sidewalk counselors.
9. Brave teachers and student leaders eager to have us share the truth about abortion to the young people in their classes.
10. Our compassionate and courageous team members, who continue to think of new and effective ways to reach out to the clinic staff and doctor in love and compassion.

The picture I'm sharing with you is just a perfect example of the beauty of Spring given to us by the Hand of God. Back in the corner of our parking lot is a beautiful tree casting dappled shadows, protecting brave little flowers eager to begin their growth spurt. What a Mighty God we serve!

"Thank You Almighty Father, that in the dark and difficult places of life, you promise Life, and Joy, and Song".

Mary

"Lord, Hear Our Prayer!"

✝ Pray for the Doctor's salvation…that he would seek God's grace and mercy

✝ Pray for the staff to realize their deep involvement, no matter what their role is inside the building

✝ Pray that the ultrasound tech shows every woman their baby on the screen

✝ Pray for all the young women in the days before their scheduled abortions, that their mind is changed

✝ Pray that each woman would confide in at least one other person…and that they would be for life.

✝ Pray that God's mercy and hope fills them before their abortion appointment, and they leave!

✝ Pray for the "already moms" that they will be moved by their other children's beauty and worth

✝ Pray for Christian men and women that choose abortion and block out the truth of God's Word

✝ Pray that even in the clinic on their abortion day, that they "wake-up" and hurry out of the building

✝ Pray for the sidewalk counselors who greet them as they come…for wisdom and courage

✝ Pray for the safety of the counselors as the threats against them have escalated

✝ Pray that Pastors care, and speak-out, and mourn the thousands of children killed

✝ Pray that the church is awakened and that they begin to yearn for abortion to be stopped

✝ Pray fervently for the men and women to find Hope in Jesus after their abortion

✝ Pray that Believers would repent of the grievous offense before God of accepting abortion